"You pose like you been doin' it forever!" Flash exclaimed.

"These will be dynamite. Let's do the next outfit."

Sam ran back into the dressing room and took off the black outfit. She slipped on the leopard-print string bikini bottoms first. Just as she was reaching for the bustier, Flash opened the curtain. Sam immediately covered her breasts with her arms.

"Modest little pigeon," Flash laughed. "Need any help?"

The SUNSET ISLAND series

Sunset Island
Sunset Kiss
Sunset Dreams

Don't miss

Sunset Farewell

coming soon!

Sunset Dreams

CHERIE BENNETT

SPLASH™

A BERKLEY / SPLASH BOOK

SUNSET DREAMS is an original publication
of The Berkley Publishing Group.
This work has never appeared before in book form.

SUNSET DREAMS

A Berkley Book / published by arrangement with
General Licensing Company, Inc.

PRINTING HISTORY
Berkley edition / August 1991

A GLC BOOK

Splash is a trademark of General Licensing Company, Inc.

ISBN: 0-425-13070-3

A BERKLEY BOOK® TM 757,375
Berkley Books are published by The Berkley Publishing Group,
200 Madison Avenue, New York, New York 10016.
The name "BERKLEY" and the "B" logo
are trademarks belonging to Berkley Publishing Corporation.

PRINTED IN THE UNITED STATES OF AMERICA

10 9 8 7 6 5 4 3 2 1

This book is for Jeff

ONE

"Samantha Bridges, you are one fine babe," Sam said to her reflection as she posed before the mirror in her room. She looked down at the *Cosmopolitan* magazine on the dresser, and changed her pose and expression to copy the cover girl's. "Incredible! Unbelievable!" she chanted at herself, trying to feel more confident.

But something was wrong. Her eyes didn't look right—not sultry enough. She closed them halfway, and tossed her head so that her long red hair shimmered around her shoulders. Much better. She leaned closer to the mirror to make sure the eye thing didn't look stupid up close, and noticed a blemish threatening to emerge on her chin.

"Oh great, that's just great," she said in disgust, dropping her pose and looking around frantically for her cover stick. "Yeah, the guy is really going to make me into a superstar with a zit popping out on my face," she muttered, trying to disguise the bump.

Okay, so I'm nervous, Sam admitted to herself. But hey, it wasn't every day that a girl got to have cocktails with a photographer from Universal Models, one of the biggest modeling agencies in the country. It was probably the most glamorous thing that had ever happened to her. *So far, anyway.*

Sam thought dreamily back to how she had first met Flash Hathaway. It had been at a party at Howie Lawrence's house. Flash had told his assistant, Leonard Fuller, to give Sam his business card. That was just before he had told Sam she should be a model. It wasn't the first time Sam had been told that. At five feet ten inches, with her long, slim frame and wild red hair, Sam had heard that line often enough. But she had never heard it from a photographer from a top modeling agency before!

"Yo, Sam, the car service is here!" one of the twins shouted up to Sam. The twins were Becky and Allie Jacobs, totally identical thirteen-year-olds whom Sam could tell apart only by the beauty mark over Allie's mouth. Sam was their au pair for the summer.

The twins' father, Dan Jacobs, had hired Sam through the National Au Pair Society. Looking after two teenagers had sounded easy enough, but the twins were so wild and precocious (for example, they had recently decided not to "date" any guys under the age of sixteen, because they'd be "way too immature") that Sam really had to watch them like a hawk. Since Sam had taken this job to have a wild summer herself, watching over "the monsters," as she had dubbed them, was not her idea of a good time.

Sam checked her reflection one last time. She had on her tiniest white Lycra miniskirt and a neon-orange bra top under a cropped white jacket. Her hair was sprayed into a huge mass of red waves and curls, and her orange matte lipstick matched the orange of her bra top. In her white high-heeled ankle boots she stood over six feet tall. *Sam, you will knock him dead*, she assured herself as she grabbed her purse off the bed.

"Wow, that outfit is way cool," Allie breathed when she saw Sam running down the stairs. "Can I borrow it sometime?"

"Nope," said Sam, retying the laces on her right boot.

"How come?" Allie whined.

"Because it's too old for you," Sam said, grabbing a jacket in case it got cold later.

"Oh, right," Becky snorted, coming up next to her sister. "*I'd* fill out that top better than you do."

Sam rolled her eyes. Unfortunately Becky was right.

The driver outside honked the horn impatiently.

"Your dad will be home in a half-hour," Sam said, checking her watch. She had arranged with Mr. Jacobs to have the evening off, and he had promised to be home at seven-thirty. "Try not to wreck the place before then."

Sam ran out the door, and Becky and Allie stuck their heads out the front door. "Hey, Sam, good luck!" one of the twins yelled.

Sam smiled back at them and gave them a wave before disappearing into the back seat of the car. They knew she was meeting an important photographer from a modeling agency. Sam was glad they'd wished her luck. Even the monsters had their occasional sweet moments.

Sam stared out the window as the car headed for Celeste's, a very upscale cocktail lounge and restaurant with a back deck overlooking the ocean. Sam had never actually been there before. But when she'd boldly called Flash to invite him out for a drink, she'd decided to name what was reportedly the most sophisticated place on the island.

Sam closed her eyes as she remembered the warning words of her friends. Both of her best friends on the island, Emma Cresswell and Carrie Alden, had called her within the past hour to warn her—*again*—about her meeting with Flash. Sam was totally exasperated with them. After all, she had just seen them that afternoon, and they'd told her enough about it then! Emma thought Flash was sleazy, and that the risks of getting involved with him outweighed the benefits. Well, that was easy for Emma to say. Emma was mega-rich, one of the Boston Cresswells. She would never have to worry about money in her whole, entire life. And Carrie had a tendency to be a real by-the-books kind of babe, a regular goody-goody. *They just don't understand me*, Sam thought as she watched the island scenery whiz by outside the window.

The sun was just beginning to set, and Sunset Island looked incredibly gorgeous. The beauty of this place made Sam feel shivery sometimes. It was so totally different from her home town, from anything she'd ever known. Sam thought back to the au pair convention in the spring in New York City, when she'd first read about Sunset Island in her au pair book. It had been described as a small, upscale summer resort off the coast of Maine, famous for everything from the dramatic architecture of its summer homes to its sandy beaches. The words *upscale* and *famous* had caught Sam's attention right away, since she planned to become both in the near future. How she would accomplish this she hadn't exactly worked out yet, but rubbing elbows with the "haves" of the world had seemed like a good start. Sunset Island had sounded like the perfect place for her.

Sam was the older of two girls in a seriously middle-class family in the tiny town of Junction, Kansas. Sam hated Junction, she hated Kansas, she hated just about everything about her life.

Sam's younger sister, Ruth Anne, loved Junction, as did her parents, and they simply did not understand Sam's yearning for great adventures in faraway places. Everybody in her family, for example, had been so pleased that she'd won a dance scholarship to Kansas State for the fall. But the idea of staying in Kansas, even going to college, made Sam's skin crawl. Surely there was more than that out there for her! *Well*, Sam said to herself as the car pulled into the circular drive in front of Celeste's, *maybe this meeting will be the first step toward my incredible future*.

After Sam paid and tipped the driver, a doorman helped Sam out of the back of the car. Sam gave him a little smile, and wondered frantically if she was supposed to tip him, too. Probably. Rich people tipped everybody. When the doorman held the door open for Sam, she gave him a dollar bill. He looked at it with amusement and handed it back to her, curling her hand around it. "Have a lovely evening, miss," he said.

Oops. Okay, so maybe she wasn't supposed to tip him. Or maybe she simply hadn't tipped him enough money, and he had returned it because he was insulted. Sam just hoped no one had seen her hand him the money and him hand it back.

"May I help you?" said the tuxedoed maître d'.

"Yes, I'm meeting Mr. Hathaway of Universal Models," Sam said in her most elegant voice. She had been practicing so that she could sound more like Emma.

"I believe Mr. Hathaway is waiting for you at the bar," the maître d' said with a small smile.

Thank God! If she had to go into the bar by herself, she didn't know what she'd do.

Sam saw Flash from across the room. Who could miss him? He had on more gold jewelry with his silk designer suit than could probably be found on all the sheiks in Kuwait. His silk shirt was unbuttoned nearly to his navel, and ten or so gold chains were lost in his forest of chest hair.

Sam sucked in her stomach and stuck out her chest, then tossed her hair back over her shoulders and headed for him. Flash smiled at her and sipped his drink, looking her up and down as she walked toward him.

"You are looking mighty fine, babe," Flash said, rising to kiss her cheek.

"Thanks," Sam said, maneuvering to sit on the stool next to him.

"Let's get a table," Flash suggested, taking her by the elbow and leading her to a tiny table in a dark corner.

"What'll you have to drink?" Flash asked her.

Emma had warned her that she wouldn't get served in a bar. But wouldn't it look totally childish to order a Coke or some juice?

"I'll have what you're having," Sam said.

Flash snapped his fingers and the waitress

came to the table. "I'll have another martini, and one for the lady," Flash said.

The waitress looked at Sam as though she was about to ask for ID. The clubs on the island tended to be very careful about checking, since there were so many underage kids on the island ready to party.

Flash winked knowingly at the waitress, who just sort of shrugged and went off to get their drinks. "She knows I'll leave her a big tip," Flash explained. "You picked a good spot, babe. Not many twinkies come in here."

"Twinkies?" Sam asked.

"The young babes, the ones who don't know the score," Flash explained. "Like if we were at the Bay View or something, you'd get carded for sure. You picked a real high-class spot." He sipped at his martini and looked her over again.

"So, Flash, how long have you been a photographer?" Sam asked. She didn't want to seem as if all she cared about was having him get her into modeling, even if it was true.

"Eons, babe," Flash said. "Universal doesn't work with just any Joe. You got to have the background, not to mention the talent."

Sam nodded. "And you sure have both, right?"

Flash grinned. "You got it. But, hey, you didn't call me to talk about my climb to the top, you want to talk about your own, am I right?"

"Right," Sam admitted.

"Good. Hey, nothin' for nothin', if you know what I mean," Flash said. "I mean, you don't go after what you want, you ain't gonna get it. You followin' me?"

Sam nodded.

"Good," Flash said, finishing off his first martini as the waitress brought over their drinks. "Here's to you," Flash said, clinking glasses with Sam. "You got a big future in this business."

Sam grinned and took a sip of her drink. Yuck! She practically spit it out, it tasted so awful. People actually drink this stuff by choice? It tasted like hair spray!

"Good martini?" Flash asked.

"Heavenly," Sam agreed as she swallowed the bitter liquid.

"Okay, assessment time," Flash said. He was giving her a look she definitely recognized. And it wasn't the sort of sexy once-over look she'd seen before. It reminded her of the hard-eyed old farmers in and around Junction. It was the exact same look she'd seen directed at livestock being considered for purchase.

"You got the height, which is the big thing," he continued. "Your figure is fine, a little small in the boob area—"

"Too small?" Sam asked nervously.

"Let's just say you ain't gonna give Dolly Parton a run for her money," Flash said, laughing at his own joke.

Sam tried to smile back. She hoped his photography was better than his sense of humor.

"Anyway, basically you're in proportion," Flash continued. "The hair is great, good bones, skin basically good, though you got a couple of craters . . ."

Oh, how humiliating. He had actually noticed her pimple! More than one pimple! Real models didn't get pimples, did they?

"The only drawback I see is your lips are kinda thin," Flash concluded. "The biggest names in the biz are all getting boob jobs and lips jobs, though, so after you make some bucks you can always invest in self-improvement," Flash added.

"After I make some bucks?" Sam echoed. "Does that mean you really think I have potential?"

"Babe, Flash Hathaway does not waste his time with the wannabes of this world. No question, you got it."

"I do?" Sam asked, totally thrilled.

Flash reached over and ran his knuckles over her hand. His diamond pinky ring scratched her skin. "All you need is some guidance. I see the po', I offer the guidance." Flash shrugged.

"So what's the first step?" Sam asked eagerly.

"Eager little bunny, huh?" Flash chuckled, finishing his martini. "Okay, the first thing we do is plan your test shots, find out how you photograph. How's tomorrow afternoon for you?"

"Tomorrow afternoon is fine," Sam said, since the twins were going to a father-daughter luncheon with their dad the next day. "But, um, I . . . don't have a lot of money," she confessed. "I mean, what do you charge?"

"Zip, *nada*, in other words it's on the house," Flash said. "Usually I charge the model for film, or for prints for her book—"

"Book?"

"Modeling book. The portfolio of photos that a model carries around with her to show how she photographs," Flash told her. "I can see you have a lot to learn, babe."

"You'll help me, though, won't you?" Sam

asked. She was suddenly afraid that Flash would think she was too much of a hick to bother with her.

"Babe, you just put yourself in my hands, know what I mean?" Flash leered. "I happen to be an excellent teacher."

Sam wasn't sure what to say to that, so she just smiled. In response to another finger-snap from Flash, the waitress brought the bill.

Sam leapt for it. After all, she had asked him out. But Flash was too quick for her. He slid it out from under her fingers.

"The pleasure is mine, sweet thing," he told her.

Secretly, Sam was relieved. The amount of the bill had surprised her; drinks were even more expensive than usual in this place.

As they walked out, Flash let his hand drop to her shoulder and Sam stiffened a little. But then he let go as he opened the door and ushered her out. *He was just trying to show me which way to go*, Sam thought. *He's kind of Hollywood; he's like that.*

Flash lived up to Sam's assessment when they got outside and he leaned over and brushed her cheek with a kiss. "See you soon, babe. I'd drop you, but I'm in a big hurry. You got a ride?"

"Oh, sure," Sam assured him, "no problem."

"See you tomorrow, gorgeous," Flash said. "Just remember, you got to think of yourself as having star quality for it to come through in the photos. Got it?"

"I got it!" Sam said, flashing her most super-starlike grin. She felt fabulous! She felt on top of the world! She felt like—

"Oh, and Sam," Flash yelled back to her, interrupting her reverie, "work on getting rid of the craters, okay, babe?"

Three people in front of the restaurant turned around to see what "craters" he was talking about.

She felt totally embarrassed. She felt like one huge zit. Looking like a superstar was not going to be easy.

TWO

"Hey, Sam, look at this!" Allie said eagerly, pushing the latest issue of *Breakers* into Sam's face.

Sam read the ad out loud as she chewed on her breakfast cereal. "'Models wanted by Cheap Boutique, Rave On, Savannah's, and the Barklay Shoppe for fashion show at Sunset Square. Girls between the ages of fifteen and twenty-two will be seen on Wednesday between ten A.M. and two P.M. in the Edwardian Room at the Sunset Inn. Some pay. No experience necessary.'

"I can imagine what 'some pay' means," Sam continued, taking a sip of her coffee. "It probably ranks somewhere between professional pencil-sharpening and nothing."

It was the morning after Sam's big meeting with Flash. She had been up half the night, dreaming about her future as a famous model. She had much bigger things on her mind than some little local fashion show. *Much*.

"I think all three of us should go," Allie decided.

"No way," Sam said. "You guys done?" she asked, ready to clear the table.

Both girls pushed their cereal bowls away, and Sam sighed. This was their idea of helping with the cleanup.

"Why 'no way'?" Becky demanded.

"First reason: you are both thirteen, not fifteen like the ad says, which makes you too young," Sam said, grabbing the cereal bowls and carrying them to the sink. "Second reason: you are both short, and everyone knows you have to be tall to be a model. Third reason: I'm going to be much too busy with the beginning of my professional modeling career to waste time on some local fashion show." Sam rinsed the bowls and stuck them in the dishwasher.

"Well, excuse me," Becky said. "I didn't realize you were such hot stuff."

"You know we could pass for fifteen, we do it all the time," Allie said. "And about the height part, I read that some models are short. They're called petites."

"Come on, take us, please, please, please, please, pretty please?" Becky wheedled.

"I'll think about it," Sam mumbled, her mind completely preoccupied with what she needed to take to her photo session.

"Jeez, she's already starting to sound like an adult," Allie said with disgust. "Dad always says, 'I'll think about it.' Let's go upstairs and call Brian and Brent." Brian and Brent were sixteen-year-old fraternal twins the girls knew from the country club. "They think we're fifteen, by the way," Allie added loftily before running upstairs with her sister.

The phone rang and Sam picked it up on the kitchen extension.

"Jacobs residence," Sam said.

"Hi, Sam. It's Carrie."

Sam heard the *click* of an extension phone being picked up upstairs.

"Becky or Allie?" Sam said with a sigh.

"Becky," Becky answered. "We need to use the phone."

"Use your own phone," Sam said, totally exasperated. The twins had their own phone line in their room, along with a phone that looked like a silver high heel.

"But then we can't both get on an extension and talk with Brian and Brent at the same time," Becky explained.

Sam could hear Carrie stifle a laugh. "Becky,

go use your own phone. That's what it's for," Sam ordered.

Becky slammed the phone down in Sam's ear.

"Unbelievable," Sam muttered. "Remind me never to have children."

"Imagine what it's like for their father when you're not around," Carrie said.

Mr. Jacobs was a single parent whose wife had run off with a younger man ages ago and hadn't been heard from since.

"I pity the guy, I really do," Sam said. "Anyhow, what's up?"

"I was just talking with Emma," Carrie said. "We were saying how exciting it is that you have this photo shoot this afternoon."

Sam had called Carrie and Emma the minute she'd gotten back from her business date with Flash the night before. She had told them every detail of the conversation, except the part about the craters.

"So we were thinking, how would you like company at the shoot?"

"You and Emma suddenly have the afternoon off?" Sam asked with surprise.

"Well, we can arrange it. No big thing," Carrie said. "I've never seen a professional modeling shoot before, and neither has Emma. It sounds great!"

"Carrie Alden, you are so full of it!" Sam said with a laugh. "You guys want to come with me because you don't trust Flash. You think it's going to be some kind of sleazoid setup, right?"

"Well, it might be a good idea to have some friends along," Carrie admitted. "It's not like you know this guy, really."

"Carrie, Flash is a photographer for Universal Models. That's the big time! He's not going to sell me into slavery or anything."

"I don't know. I was just talking to Billy and he says that Flash doesn't have the best rep in the world."

Carrie was referring to Billy Sampson, her new boyfriend. Billy was incredibly nice and incredibly cute, with long hair and one pierced ear. He was also the lead singer of a very hot local band, Flirting with Danger.

"Well, neither do you and Billy, after your little fun-filled nude beach party," Sam pointed out.

Just a few days before, Carrie and Billy, along with a ton of other people, had been picked up by the police at a beach party. Carrie had been trying to act sophisticated and cool, because that was what she thought Billy wanted, so she had stripped to go skinny-dipping just like most everyone else. Unfortunately some neighbor had called the police, and

19

Carrie wound up in the police station, completely mortified. As it turned out, Billy liked Carrie because she was natural, smart, and sincere. He'd had no part in the drinking or the drugs at the party, and he'd kept his clothes on. But rumors had gotten started, and it seemed like everyone on the island was gossiping about what had happened at that party.

"Hey, that's not fair and you know it," Carrie objected.

"Of course it's not. That's my point," Sam said. "Just because Flash has a bad reputation doesn't mean he earned it."

"Okay, I see what you mean," Carrie conceded. "But we'd still like to go with you for fun, honest."

"Well, then, honestly, I'd love to have you come," Sam said. "The truth is, I'm kind of nervous. Can you guys come over early and help me decide what to wear and what to take, stuff like that?"

"I can be over at two o'clock," Carrie said. "Claudia and Graham are taking the kids on a picnic, and they gave me the day off. They're trying to spend extra time together as a family before Graham leaves on tour again." Carrie had the unbelievable good fortune to be the au pair for the Templetons, or, as they were more commonly known to the world, rock superstar Graham Perry and his wife, Claudia.

"Great," Sam said. "I'll call Emma."

"You don't need to. I already told her we'd meet at your house at two unless you absolutely refused to let us come," Carrie admitted.

"You guys cooked this whole thing up, didn't you?" Sam said with a laugh.

"Hey, what are friends for?" Carrie said. "See you soon!"

By the time Carrie and Emma showed up, Sam had every outfit she owned either on her bed or on the floor. She was putting on a third coat of black mascara when they walked in.

"It looks like someone dropped a bomb in here," Carrie remarked, walking around a pile of clothes.

"Hello to you, too," Sam said. "Is the mascara glopping up on my right eye?"

"It's okay," Emma said, scrutinizing Sam's lashes. "But why are you putting on makeup before a photo shoot?"

"Emma, don't you know that top models wear tons of makeup to achieve that natural look?" Sam said. "They wear, like, three shades of blush and contour just to look like they have a healthy glow."

"Bleah!" said Carrie, who rarely wore any makeup at all. "That would drive me nuts."

"What I meant was that usually models show up at shoots with no makeup on," Emma explained. "Then the photographer tells the makeup artist what look he wants, and the models' makeup is done by a professional." Emma knew a little about the modeling business. A few of the younger supermodels had been classmates of hers at Aubergame, her exclusive Swiss boarding school. They were always getting excused from classes to jet off to one fashion show or shoot after another.

Sam stopped with the mascara wand midway to her eye. "You think he'd actually have a makeup artist there?" she asked. "Naw," she said, answering her own question. "He's doing the shots for free, so I think it's a safe bet I have to do my own makeup."

"That's another thing," Carrie said, moving over a pile of clothes so she could sit on the rug. "What's in it for him?"

Sam sighed. "So young and yet so cynical."

"I'm serious!" Carrie said.

"Well, then, for your information, it's like I told you. He thinks I can be a really, really big model. Then he can say he discovered me, and then we both make a fortune."

"Are you sure?" Carrie asked skeptically.

"Hey, I'm a walking gold mine," Sam said, finishing her makeup. "How do I look?"

"Great," Emma told her.

"Yeah, great," Carrie echoed, trying to be supportive.

"Tell me the truth," Sam asked them. "Can you see my pimples?"

"What pimples?" Emma asked her.

"Two on my chin," Sam said. "I've got about ten layers of coverup over them. I swear to God, I'm going to be old enough to have lines on my face and I'll still be getting zits."

"Well, I can't see any," Emma said.

"Aren't you overreacting a little?" Carrie asked her.

"Are you kidding?" Sam said, stuffing clothes into a duffel bag. "Models have to look perfect."

"No, they don't," Emma disagreed. "In the first place, they're made up to look perfect. Then the photographer shoots them so they look even more perfect."

"And then after the photos are developed, some artist airbrushes everything so it looks impossibly perfect," Carrie finished.

"Should I take this yellow tank top or does it make my tan look greenish?" Sam asked, completely ignoring her friends' remarks. She looked at her watch. "Oh, wow, it's late. We gotta go. I'll just take everything," she said, stuffing the rest of the pile of clothes into her bag.

Carrie had borrowed the Templetons' Mercedes, and ten minutes later the girls were at Flash's studio. It was on the second floor of an older office building in the small downtown section of the island.

When the girls got off the elevator, loud rock music blasted toward them like a wall of sound. At the far end of the room huge lights were set up around a giant pale blue roll of paper hung from the ceiling to create a seamless backdrop running all the way to the floor. There were cameras and mirrors all over, and various accessories and props were draped over every surface. Magazine spreads and photos of famous and not-so-famous models were taped up all over the room.

"I've died and gone to heaven," Sam murmured, but of course no one heard her over the music.

Across the long loftlike room Emma saw a short, chubby blond guy setting up a light, and her heart sank. It was Leonard, Flash's assistant, whom she had danced with at Howie Lawrence's party. The experience had been a nightmare. Leonard was the worst dancer Emma had ever seen—ostentatiously bad, with no concept of how excruciatingly, embarrassingly horrible he looked. In fact, he prided himself on his dancing. Emma had been much too polite to clue him in.

As if on cue, Leonard saw Emma and his eyes lit up. He boogied across the room to Emma, apparently trying to keep time to the music but failing miserably.

"Babe!" he screamed in Emma's ear. "I was hoping I'd see you!"

"Nice to see you, too," Emma managed to respond politely.

"Here, let me help you with that," Leonard bellowed, grabbing the duffel bag from Sam. "Walk this way!" he screamed, then danced unrhythmically toward a door at the other end of the room.

Sam looked at Emma and shrugged, then she "walked" behind Leonard, dancing exactly as he was dancing. Emma and Carrie fell in behind her, until a parade of bad dancers was boogieing across the room, three of them giggling hysterically.

Leonard ushered them into Flash's office, where the photographer was sitting behind a desk looking at some contact sheets through a loupe.

"Sam! Babe!" Flash said, coming around the

desk to kiss her cheek. "What's with the goop?" he asked her, staring at her face.

"The makeup?" Sam asked. Her voice faltered. "I . . . I thought I was supposed to come prepared."

"Scrape the palette, babe. There's some makeup remover in the dressing room. Belinda's gotta be able to see what she's working with."

The door opened and a tall young woman with moussed-up blond hair and an angry expression stuck her head in. "Which one of you?" she asked.

"That's Belinda, your makeup artist," Flash said. "The tall one's all yours, Beli."

"I told you not to call me that," Belinda snapped. She looked Sam over. "Go into the makeup room next door and clean off your face," she said, sounding thoroughly bored. She pointed Sam in the right direction and then left, shaking her head.

"You I met at Howie's bash," Flash said, pointing to Emma, "and you I remember from the recording studio thing, am I right?"

"Right," Carrie said.

"Flash Hathaway never forgets a great bod, Car," Flash said, looking Carrie over appreciatively. "From the neck down you got that

Marilyn Monroe kind of thing happening." He turned to Emma. "As for you, blondie, you look like the type who never sweats, even in the clinch, if you catch my drift."

"No," said Emma in her frostiest voice, "I haven't a clue as to your drift." There were some advantages to having grown up with a mother like hers after all, if it could help put a jerk in his place. Normally Emma hated to speak that way, but this Flash character was worth the exception.

"Ha," Flash barked. "Classy babe. So, can I get you girls a Coke? A smoke? A toke?" he said, adding a wink.

Carrie and Emma both managed to decline politely.

"Let's go see if Sam needs any help," Carrie suggested.

"He is the biggest sleaze I've ever met in my life," Emma hissed when she and Carrie were out of Flash's office. "How did he ever get to work for Universal Models?"

Carrie shrugged. "Maybe he takes great pictures, although it's hard to imagine." Carrie was quite a fine photographer herself. In fact, she planned to become a photojournalist one day. She hated to think that anyone as idiotic as Flash could actually succeed in her chosen profession.

"I say we stick close to Sam," Emma whispered. "I really do not trust this guy."

"Ditto," Carrie said.

When they joined Sam and Belinda in the makeup room, Sam's makeup was almost done.

"Wow, that looks fabulous," Emma said.

Belinda had done a very natural-looking makeup on Sam. Although she had on a thoroughly concealing base, her eye makeup was all neutrals. Sam actually looked less made up than when she did it herself, but at the same time all her best features were highlighted.

"You're really talented," Carrie told Belinda.

"Thanks," said Belinda as she combed Sam's eyebrows up with a tiny comb. Then she took a huge brush and dipped it into loose translucent powder, knocked most of the powder off, and brushed it across Sam's face. "This sets the makeup," Belinda explained. She stood back to look at Sam's face in the mirror.

"You sure I don't need more . . . color or something?" Sam asked. She wasn't used to seeing her makeup look this natural.

Belinda just raised her eyebrows at Sam's comment.

"I love it!" said Carrie. "Maybe you could show me how you do that some time," she suggested hopefully. "I mean, it looks so un-made-up."

Belinda looked at Carrie. "What do you do for a living?"

"I'm an au pair," Carrie said, taken aback.

"That means you babysit, right?" Belinda asked.

"Sort of," Carrie said.

"So would I ask you to come over and babysit for my kids for free just because you're good at it?" she demanded.

Carrie bit her lip. "No, I guess not."

"Let's go look at your clothes," Belinda said to Sam. "I get to play stylist, too."

Sam shrugged at her friends and followed Belinda out of the makeup room.

"I thought she was going to bite my head off," Carrie said.

"I don't like any of this," Emma said, narrowing her eyes. "Come on, we're going into the dressing room."

"And have her yell at me again? No, thanks," Carrie said.

"Listen, if there's one thing I've learned from my dear mother, it's how to act imperious when necessary," Emma said firmly. She dragged Carrie toward the door marked Dressing Room, knocked lightly, and went in.

"What do you think?" Sam asked. "This is the outfit Belinda said I should wear first."

Belinda, thank heavens, was nowhere to be seen. Sam had on a short pink pleated shirt, lime-green polka-dot crop top, and her red cowboy boots. Her long red hair was in a ponytail on top of her head and tied with a orange-and-black polka-dot scarf.

"It's . . . awfully bright, isn't it?" Carrie asked uncertainly.

Sam shrugged. "I'd never wear this stuff together, that's all I can say."

Flash stuck his head in the dressing room. "Great look, babe," he enthused.

"Really?" Sam asked. "Isn't it a little, uh, colorful?"

"We're doing a color test first," Flash explained.

"And about my hair," Sam said, feeling for the ponytail that sprouted out of the top of her head. "I look like Woody Woodpecker."

"Come on out here," Flash said. "Let me show you something."

The girls walked back out into the main room. Flash pointed to a photo spread from a major fashion magazine taped to the wall. The models all had on riotous color combinations. What seemed to clash in real life just looked lively in the photos. To add to the playful atmosphere, the models were all jumping around energetically.

"Well?" Flash demanded.

"It looks great," Sam admitted.

"It paid great, too," Flash said, "Do me a favor. Don't question my decisions, okay, babe? Because if you question my decisions we are going to have a hard time working together."

"No, I wasn't. I mean, I won't," Sam said hastily.

"Great," Flash said. "Let's go for it. Leonard, crank up the Janet!"

"You got it, boss!" Leonard yelled. Janet Jackson's latest single came blaring through the sound system.

"Just one last thing before we start," Flash said. "You gotta sign a release form."

Flash brandished a printed form and a pen at Sam.

"What's that?" Sam screamed over the music.

"It just means you're giving me permission to take the shots, babe. I do everything totally on the up and up."

Sam looked doubtful. The form seemed full of complicated language, and it was hard to concentrate with the music blasting.

"All models sign releases. No release, no photos," Flash yelled when he saw her hesitate.

Sam started to sign the form.

"Wait!" Carrie said. "Don't you think you should read it first?"

Sam faltered. "I *should* read it," she told Flash.

"Leonard, turn off the Janet!" Flash screamed.

The silence in the room seemed deafening.

"Look," Flash said, "I think this was a bad idea. Frankly, I'm hurt you don't trust me. I can't be babysitting you through this. I am doing you a big favor here, a *big* favor. This is just not gonna work out. No hard feelings." Flash took the release form from Sam and started back to his office.

"Wait!" Sam called to him. "I'm sorry. I'm just nervous. I'll sign it."

"Sam—" Emma began.

"I'll *sign* it," Sam repeated, shutting Emma up. She twirled Carrie around by her shoulder and leaned on her back to sign the paper.

"Great," said Flash with a grin. "Now, let's get to work!"

Leonard put the music back on. Flash placed Sam on the light blue paper, then turned all the lights on her.

"Move to the music, babe!" Flash instructed Sam.

At first she felt nervous and self-conscious, and moved her arms and legs awkwardly.

"You look gorgeous through this lens, babe, honest-to-God luscious. Loosen up!"

The more Flash called encouragement to Sam, the better she felt. Her friends smiled at her.

"Fabulous, babe! Jump around! Dance! Go crazy!" Flash yelled, clicking away.

With the hot beat of the music in her ears and her friends smiling at her for support, suddenly Sam got into it. She danced around sexily, throwing her hair around her head. She did every pose she'd ever practiced in her mirror, and added a few new ones for good measure.

"Unbelievable!" Flash yelled when the song finished. "Okay, go change into the bikini," he ordered.

"Belinda said the pink one," Sam said.

"Great, babe. These shots are gonna be dynamite!"

Carrie and Emma crowded into the dressing room with Sam while she changed.

"I told you this was going to be totally cool," Sam said, taking her hair out of the ponytail.

"You need more powder," Belinda said, sticking her head in the door.

"Oh! I didn't realize you were still here," Sam said, adjusting the top of her bathing suit.

Belinda didn't say anything; she just powdered Sam down, changed her lipstick to a pink shade that matched her bathing suit, and disappeared again.

"What a sweetheart," Sam said, making a face. She turned to her friends. "How do I look?"

"Gorgeous," Sam said.

"Thin," Carrie sighed.

"Yeah, like you're fat," Sam scoffed. "You're curvy. I'd kill for a set of lungs like yours."

"A set of lungs?" Carrie repeated. "Now there's a colorful expression."

Sam danced out under the hot lights again and immediately threw herself into the music. Now that she could see everything really was under control, she felt fabulous.

"I love it, babe! I love it!" Flash yelled. "Gimme a little more tease. Oh yeah, that's the look!"

Sam gave him her half-closed-eyes look and licked her lips. She turned around and posed looking over one shoulder. She held her hair up on top of her head with both hands and posed with one hip sticking out.

"You're a natural," Flash said after Sam had posed through two more songs. He turned off the bright lights. "I think we got some great stuff."

Sam threw her arms around Flash and gave him a spontaneous hug. "Oh, I loved it!" she cried.

"Great, babe," Flash said, patting her behind. "I'll call you when the contact sheet is ready."

Sam was hyper as she changed and packed up her stuff. "This is only the beginning, you guys! I can't wait to see the shots. I told you I could handle Flash. He was totally cool."

"You call that hand on your butt just now totally cool?" Carrie asked Sam.

"That was merely a friendly thing," Sam scoffed. "After all, I hugged him," she pointed out. She looked around the dressing room to see if she had forgotten anything. "You want to go over to the Play Café? I'm starved."

"I have to get back," Emma said, looking at her watch. "I promised Katie I'd watch a video with her."

"Thanks for coming, you guys," Sam said as they walked to the car. "It made me much more comfortable. And now you won't be so flipped out next time I go there minus the chaperones."

Emma and Carrie exchanged a glance. They weren't nearly as sure about Flash as Sam was.

THREE

"Okay, how do we look?" Becky asked Sam. She and Allie stood in Sam's room wearing identical jean miniskirts, tight black T-shirts, and black spike heels. Makeup was piled thickly on their faces, and their long brown hair was sprayed up to an astounding height.

"Frightening," Sam said, putting down the fashion magazine she was reading.

It was the morning after Sam's photo shoot, and after endless cajoling the night before, she had finally agreed that she would take the twins to the modeling call for the fashion show.

"I'm telling them the truth about how old you are, though," Sam had warned them. "No way am I lying for you. If they want you anyway, and if your dad says it's okay, then fine."

"Oh, get a life, Sam," Allie had scoffed. "In

37

modeling no one cares how old you really are; they just care how old you look. Unless of course you're over the hill completely, like, I don't know, twenty-five or something."

Now they were all decked out for their interview, eager for Sam's approval. It was not forthcoming.

"What do you mean, frightening?" Beck demanded in a wounded voice.

"It took us hours to perfect this," Allie added.

Sam sighed. "First of all, lose the black spikes. They look slutty. Where did you get heels like that, anyway?"

"We've got lots of stuff you don't know about," Becky smirked. "Anyway, I like the shoes."

"Do you want my opinion as a professional, or not?" Sam asked them.

"Okay," Becky finally decided. Allie nodded in agreement.

"Change to flats," Sam instructed. "Wear a looser T-shirt, brush your hair, and wipe off most of the makeup."

"We'll look like little kids!" Allie protested.

"You will look very pretty," Sam said. "You guys have beautiful hair, pretty faces, nice figures, great skin. Right now you are, as my mother says, gilding the lily."

"*You* wear a lot of makeup sometimes," Allie said slyly. "What does your mother say to you?"

"I don't have to listen to my mother because I am an adult!" Sam told them. "I'm just trying to help you."

"Really? Are you sure you're not saying that because you want us to look like babies?" Becky asked.

"Yeah," said Allie. "I think you just don't want the competition."

"Oh, get real, Allie," Sam scoffed. The twins stared at her defiantly. Sam could see the insecurity underneath their bravado. "Look," she said in a much kinder tone of voice, "how about I help you guys pick something out, and I fix your hair and makeup?"

"Would you?" Allie asked quickly. "I mean, I think that would be okay," she added, looking over at her sister and trying to sound cool.

"Sure," Sam said. "Come on."

A half-hour later Sam stepped back and looked at the twins. They looked great. They still had on their jean skirts, but with them they wore oversized pink T-shirts and white summer flats. Their hair was freshly brushed, and they had on just enough makeup to enhance their natural good looks.

"I don't like it," Allie said, getting into the car. "I think we look like Bettys."

"What's a Betty?" Sam asked, backing out of the driveway.

"Betty the baton twirler," Allie explained, rolling her eyes. "One of those rah-rah types who say 'golly' and 'gee wiz.'"

"Truly barfy." Becky shuddered meaningfully.

"Well, you don't look like Bettys," Sam said. "You look great."

When they got to the Edwardian Room at the Sunset Inn, it was teeming with girls.

"Sign up here," said a middle-aged woman sitting behind a desk.

"These girls are only thirteen," Sam said right away.

Allie and Becky stood behind Sam, fuming with complete mortification.

The woman shrugged. "Half the girls here could be, for all I know. As long as they're mature enough, have the right look, and get their parents' permission, it doesn't really matter."

"Oh, we're very mature," Becky assured her.

"Good for you, dear," the woman said. She handed Becky and Allie application blanks, marked in the top right-hand corner with numbers fifty-six and fifty-seven.

"Oh, and here's yours," the woman said, handing an application to Sam. "Be sure to sign up, dear."

"I'm not applying," Sam said loftily. "I'm a professional."

"Too bad for us," the woman said. "Next."

Sam sat with the two girls to help them with their applications.

"Height: five feet two inches," Becky said as she wrote on her application form. "Weight. We have to tell them our weight?"

"Lie," Allie advised. Both girls scribbled something on the application.

"Dress size," Becky read. Both girls wrote size five. "Is that too big?" Becky asked Sam, biting on the eraser of her pencil.

"Why, Sammi darlin', how ducky to run into you!" drawled a sickeningly sweet voice with a Southern accent.

Sam looked up at the face of the she-witch Sam most loved to hate, Lorell Courtland. Sam had had the misfortune to meet Lorell way back at the au pair convention in New York. All Lorell had done was brag about how much money her family had. For example, she had made sure the world knew that she had flown in to the convention from Atlanta on her father's private jet. It was incredibly nauseating. No one had hired Lorell as an au pair, clearly because her odious personality was all too obvious. So her father had arranged for her to live with the Popes, friends of the family, for the summer, allegedly to be a role model for their twelve-year-old daughter, Alexa.

As usual, Lorell looked perfect. Her straight black hair was cropped in a chin-length bob and pushed behind one diamond-studded ear. Today she wore a cream-colored silk shirt and matching skirt. Sam could tell that the skirt alone cost more than her own entire wardrobe.

With Lorell, of course, was her entourage, Daphne Whittinger and Diana De Witt. Daphne was an extremely thin, very high-strung girl who tried—and failed—to copy Lorell's every move. Diana had gone to boarding school with Emma, and they loathed each other. In fact, Diana had only shown up on Sunset Island when Lorell called her and told her that Emma was pretending to be poor so that she could, as Diana had put it, "mix with the masses." Diana had flown in from Boston to blow Emma's cover. And as if that hadn't been enough, she had brought with her Trent Hayden-Bishop III, Emma's past-tense, sort-of boyfriend, cleverly if evilly managing to stage the entire confrontation in front of Emma's new boyfriend, hunky swimming instructor Kurt Ackerman. Well, that had almost destroyed Emma's relationship with Kurt. It was really all very complicated. The bottom line was that these three girls were absolutely, totally, and utterly detestable.

"Ducky to see you, too," Sam said in an equally insincere imitation of Lorell's outrageously insincere tone.

"Hey, Sam, I don't know my measurements," Allie said. "What should I put down?"

"These must be the little girls you're working for this summer," Lorell said in her nauseatingly sweet voice.

"*Little* girls?" Becky said dangerously, shooting Lorell a deadly look.

"Why, aren't they jes' darlin'?" Lorell purred. "They look exactly alike!"

"Darling," Daphne agreed, trying to copy Lorell's expression.

It was fortunate that neither Lorell nor Daphne bothered to make eye contact with the objects of their obnoxious attentions, Sam thought. Because the looks on the twins' faces would have turned them to stone.

"Where's Emma and what's-her-name?" Diana asked.

"I imagine Emma and Carrie are working, which is exactly what I'm doing right now," Sam said pointedly. She turned to Allie. "Just leave the part about your measurements blank," she advised.

"Well, I guess *you* have the height to model," Lorell said, looking Sam over skeptically. "What do you think, Diana?"

"The height is good," Diana said, nodding seriously. "But Sam, you don't mind some constructive criticism, do you? Well, your look is really—how can I put this?—kind of tacky. You know, really low-class. On the other hand, how *could* you have known?" Her eyes scanned Sam's ripped jeans, white T-shirt, and cotton vest.

"Thank you, Diana," Sam said, wide-eyed. "You know, in Kansas we really have no stores or anything. People weave their own clothes from cornhusks."

Diana, Lorell, and Daphne laughed. "Isn't she funny?" Lorell asked her friends. "I mean, in a buffoonish sort of way?"

"Hey, Lorell, you have to sign up now or it's going to be too late," Daphne pointed out, raking her hand nervously through her thin blond hair.

"Go sign us up, Daphne," Lorell ordered her

friend. Daphne scampered off to do her bidding.

"You know, Lorell, you ought to model that fabulous bathing suit you got at the Cheap Boutique," Sam said wickedly. "I mean, it is so . . . so *you*."

Sam and Carrie had been at the Cheap Boutique recently and had pretended to fight over a truly ugly, tacky leopard-print bathing suit just so that Lorell would want to buy it. Sure enough, it had worked. And Lorell, who usually dressed to perfection, was later seen strutting around the beach in this monstrosity, that made her breasts look like traffic cones.

"Oh, I gave that suit to Daphne," Lorell said casually. "What could I do? She begged."

"Here are the applications, you guys," Daphne said breathlessly handing one to Lorell and one to Diana.

"Where's yours?" Sam asked Daphne.

"Me?" Daphne squeaked. "I'm much too fat to model," she said in a horrified voice.

Sam looked at Daphne to see if she was serious. Daphne was almost painfully thin. In fact, it seemed to Sam that Daphne was thinner every time she ran into her.

"You know what they say," Diana cooed. "You can never be too rich or too thin. Right, Sam?"

"I wouldn't know," Sam said.

"I guess that's right. You wouldn't, would you?" Diana observed. "But look on the bright side. At least you're thin!"

"Let's go, girls," Lorell said. "Best of luck to you and your kiddies, Sam!"

Allie and Becky, who had been listening to this entire exchange, stood up and faced Lorell and her friends.

"For your information," Allie said, "we are not kiddies."

"Yeah," said Becky, "and also for your information, Sam isn't applying for this fashion show because she's a real professional model."

"Since when?" Lorell asked.

"Since she just did her first professional photo shoot," Allie informed her.

"She's going to be a famous model for Universal Models, and she's going to be in magazines and stuff," Becky finished.

Lorell was dumbstruck for a moment. "Universal Models? Wait a minute: tell me you didn't pose for Flash Hathaway."

"What if I did?" Sam asked.

Lorell made a big show of laughing so hard she practically fell over. "Please! Flash hits on every new girl on this island! Daphne told me all about him!"

Daphne nodded eagerly, thrilled to be in on something for once. "Every summer he chooses some new girl," said Daphne. "He takes pictures of her, then he tries to get into her pants," she finished triumphantly.

Lorell laughed. "Well, I guess in Sam's case that shouldn't be too difficult."

Lorell turned away, still laughing, Diana and Daphne trailing behind her. Allie and Becky just stood there in a state of shock.

"Look up *three-headed she-devil from hell* in the dictionary, and you will find their picture," Sam said.

"Do you think it's true about Flash?" Allie asked Sam anxiously.

"Of course not," Sam scoffed. "They're just jealous. Professional models have to put up with that sort of thing all the time."

The twins nodded. To them, Sam was the ultimate in hip.

But inside, Sam's heart was racing. Maybe it really was true. Maybe Flash had no intention of helping her to become a professional model. Maybe she just didn't have what it took.

"Numbers fifty-six and fifty-seven!" a loud voice called out.

"That's us!" Allie said, jumping up.

Sam shepherded Becky and Allie into the

47

cordoned-off area where four women and one man were seated behind a table interviewing the applicants.

"Hi, girls, I'm Pamela Winslow," said an extremely attractive, tall, and slender middle-aged woman. "I'm in charge of hiring the models for the Sunset Square fashion show." Her face looked familiar to Sam, but Sam didn't know why. "The other people you see here are representatives from the stores participating in the show," Ms. Winslow continued. "Please, have a seat."

Allie and Becky sat opposite Ms. Winslow, who looked up at Sam questioningly. "I only have two applications here."

"Oh, I'm not applying," Sam explained. "I'm just here with them. They're only thirteen."

Ms. Winslow smiled. "So I see."

"Does that mean we're out?" Allie asked in a resigned voice.

"Well, it is a little young," Ms. Winslow said, "but two adorable identical twins in the show might be a great idea." She looked over at the store representatives, who nodded enthusiastically.

"I'd love to have them in some really cute junior things from my store," said a heavyset woman with a friendly face. "I own Savannah's," she added.

"And those little shorts sets I'm showing in Day-Glo colors would be darling on them," another said, nodding. "We could have them come out together in the same outfit, but in different colors."

The twins bobbed their heads like crazy.

"My concern is whether or not you're old enough to be reliable and professional about this," Ms. Winslow said.

"Oh, we are!" Allie assured her.

"Maybe I should ask your sister," Ms. Winslow said, looking over at Sam.

"Oh, I'm not their sister, Ms. Winslow," Sam corrected.

"Please, call me Pam."

"Could you excuse me a minute, Pam?" Becky said politely. She walked over to Sam and whispered in her ear, "I will die if you say you're our babysitter."

"I'm . . . an older friend," Sam explained as Becky took her seat again. "They are, um, mature for their age. But they haven't asked their father's permission yet."

"Well, here's the parental permission form he has to sign. It gives all the information," Pam said, handing the form to Sam. "The pay is a flat fee of twenty-five dollars, including all fittings, rehearsals, and the show itself. The signed form needs to be dropped off at the Cheap Boutique tomorrow."

Becky, Allie, and Sam said good-bye and walked back out into the main room.

"Oh my God, we're going to be models!" Becky squealed to her sister. They both screamed and started jumping up and down, hugging each other.

"Your father didn't say yes yet," Sam reminded them.

"Excuse me, could I speak with you a moment?" It was Pamela Winslow, standing next to Sam.

"Sure," Sam said. "Wait right here," Sam told the twins. She followed Pam over to a private corner of the room.

"I just wondered if you might reconsider being in the fashion show," Pam said. "You have a wonderful look."

"I do?" Sam said, totally thrilled.

Pamela Winslow nodded. "I used to model for Mega Models," she said, naming one of the most prestigious modeling agencies in the world. "I still do, occasionally."

Sam's eyes lit up. "That's why I recognized your face! I've seen your picture in *Town and Country*, and *Harper's Bazaar*, too, right?"

"Right," Pam said. "I don't do as much print

as I used to, but I keep my hand in. Now I do a lot of live fashion shows around the country, choosing the models, emceeing the show, that sort of thing."

Sam nodded enthusiastically.

"The thing is, I don't see someone with your potential every day," Pam told her seriously.

"Actually, I just did my first professional test shots for Universal Models!" Sam said.

"So don't you think this fashion show would be good experience for you?" Pam asked.

"Well, to tell you the truth, the idea of modeling in an amateur fashion show—no offense but I think—it might hurt my professional reputation."

"I see," Pam said carefully. She looked as if she wanted to say something more to Sam, but she remained silent. "Well, if you change your mind, here's my card," she said finally, handing Sam an ivory-colored business card with raised navy lettering.

"What did she want?" the twins demanded when Sam returned to them. "Did she decide we were too young after all?" Allie asked.

"It had nothing to do with you, actually," Sam told them. "She wanted to tell me that I should be a professional model. I told her I already was," she said coolly as they walked to the car.

"Wow, that is awesome," Becky breathed.

"Yeah, I guess the three-headed she-devil from hell didn't know what it was talking about after all," Allie giggled.

"I guess it didn't at that," Sam said.

FOUR

It was Friday, two days later. Sam was up to her elbows in soapy water, scrubbing the burnt gunk off the bottom of a pot the monsters had left on the stove too long, when the phone rang.

"Can somebody get that?" Sam screamed.

They had just returned from the twins' first fitting for the fashion show. Sam had made a deal with them that if she talked their dad into letting them be in the show, they would be more helpful around the house.

The phone rang again.

"Get the freaking phone!" Sam yelled.

"We're busy!" one of the twins yelled back from upstairs.

"I am going to knock their little heads together," Sam seethed as she quickly dried her hands and ran for the phone.

"Hello?" she practically barked into the receiver.

"I am about to make your day," Carrie chirped happily. "No, no, don't thank me. Just tell me you aren't busy tonight."

"I'm not," Sam said. "Mr. Jacobs is dating some woman who he wants to introduce to Allie and Becky. So it's sort of a Jacobs family get-together night. Can you imagine this poor woman becoming the monsters' stepmother? Do you think I should warn her?"

"Aren't you even a teensy bit interested in my big news?" Carrie asked.

"Sorry, I've got the murder of two juveniles on my mind. What's up?"

"I have a date with Billy tonight," Carrie began.

"That's nice," Sam said.

"And Emma has a date with Kurt tonight," Carrie continued.

"Great, I'm happy for you both. I'll be sitting home staring at the walls. Or I guess I could go to the Play Café by myself—" Sam mused.

"Wait, I'm not done," Carrie interrupted. "You have a date with Pres Travis!"

"I what?" Sam asked.

Pres—actually, his real name was Presley—was the incredibly sexy and muscular bass player for Flirting with Danger. Sam had been flirting with him since day one, but he hadn't actually asked for her phone number or anything.

"All six of us are going out!" Carrie said. "Billy and Pres have their van, everyone has the night off—"

"Slow down," Sam commanded. "How is it that I have a date with Pres and he didn't ask me?"

"Well, I was talking with Billy, and I mentioned that you kind of liked Pres, and he mentioned that Pres kind of liked you back, and one thing led to another, and well, I kind of fixed the whole thing up. We're picking you up at eight!"

"But I *kind of* don't go out with a guy unless he actually asks me out," Sam said.

"In that case it would behoove you to get off the phone," Carrie laughed.

"He's really going to call me?" Sam asked. "He's, like, the hottest guy on the entire island!"

"That is entirely a matter of opinion," Carrie said, laughing again. "See you later!"

As soon as Sam hung up the phone, it rang again.

"Hello?"

"Hey, Sam, it's Pres." Pres had the greatest voice, a soft, sexy Tennessee twang.

"Hey, yourself," Sam said back easily. She was so glad Carrie had warned her that he was going to call. Her heart was only beating double time instead of quadruple time.

Sam heard the extension phone being picked up. *Oh, just terrific.* Now *the twins are getting the phone.*

"It's for me," said Sam.

"Is it a guy?" one of the twins asked.

"Wait a sec, sweetheart, let me check," Pres drawled.

That cracked the twins up completely, but they did finally hang up.

"Sorry," Sam said.

"No prob," Pres laughed. "I've got a little sister. How you doin'?"

"Fine. How's the band?" Sam asked.

"Things are hoppin' for us, but I can tell you about that when I see you. That is, *if* I can see you. I thought maybe we could hang out with Billy and Carrie and Emma and Kurt tonight."

"Sounds great," Sam said.

"Cool. We've got the van. So, we'll be by about eight, okay?"

"Great!" Sam said. "See you then."

Yes! She had a date with Pres!

Sam ran upstairs to look through her wardrobe. Although she hadn't said anything, she was privately a little ticked that both Emma and Sam had found boyfriends before she had. Not that she begrudged them their happiness or anything, but *she* was supposed to be the hot one. How could she be the hot one if she wasn't even dating anybody?

"Black cotton skirt? No. Lace tights? No. White Lycra number? Overkill. Let's see . . ."

"Do you have a date?" Becky asked, bouncing into Sam's room.

"Thank you so much for knocking," Sam said.

"So, do you?"

"Yes, as matter of fact," Sam said. "Purple fishnet hose? Tacky," she continued.

"Who is he?" Becky asked.

"His name is Presley," Sam said absently, still pawing through her clothes.

"Wait a second," said Becky. "There's only one guy on this island named Presley, and he's the bass player for Flirting with Danger, and you do not have a date with him."

"Yes, I do."

"No way," Becky said.

"Well, if you're here tonight at eight o'clock, you can see for yourself," Sam said.

"Omigod, omigod, they are, like, our favorite band in the entire world. *Omigod!*" Becky ran to the door of Sam's room. "Allie!" she screamed. "Come here! You are not going to believe this!"

"What?" said Allie, sticking her head out of the door of the twins' bedroom. She had on garish purple lipstick and eyeshadow. "I'm experimenting with a new look. Do you like it?"

"Sam has a date with Presley from Flirting with Danger!" Becky said, grabbing Allie's hand.

"No!" Allie screeched. "He's coming to our house? Presley is going to be actually breathing in our house?"

"Billy Sampson, too," Sam said. "He's dating my friend Carrie. But I don't think they're actually coming in the house. It's a *date*. You know, where we go *out*."

Both girls screamed at once.

"What time are they coming over?" Allie asked. "Because we absolutely have to be here."

"Around eight," Sam said.

"No! It can't be eight!" Becky moaned tragically. We're supposed to leave here at seven to go meet Dad's new girlfriend!"

"Well, I guess you'll meet Pres and Billy another time, then."

"Are you kidding? How do we know Pres will ever ask you out again? We've *got* to be here!" Allie shrieked.

"Thank you for that vote of confidence," Sam said, still staring into her closet. "Okay, jeans. I'm going to wear jeans," she decided. "I look good in jeans, and it won't look like I'm trying too hard, right?"

"Wear jeans and he'll definitely never ask you out again," Becky advised. "You should get all dressed up in some babe clothes."

"Babe clothes?" Sam asked.

"Short, sexy, and see-through," Becky advised.

"Why am I asking a thirteen-year-old what I should wear on a date?" Sam wondered out loud.

"Whatever you do, don't tell him we're thirteen!" Allie pleaded.

"Actually, I don't think you'll be a major topic of conversation," Sam told her.

"So? We don't care. We have our own dates tomorrow night," Becky said.

"You're not allowed to date yet," Sam said.

"We're allowed to go to parties," Becky said. "Brenda Clauser is having a party and we happen to have dates with Brian and Brent," she boasted.

Sam knew who Brenda Clauser was. The kid was really bad news. Carrie had told her that Brenda had babysat for Ian when they had all been at the Graham Perry concert. When Carrie had gotten home after midnight, four-year-old Chloe was all alone upstairs. Thirteen-year-old Brenda had been in the pool in the basement with twelve-year-old Ian, and she was swimming in revealing wet underwear.

"Brian and Brent are sixteen," Sam said.

"So?" Allie said defiantly.

"Isn't that a little old for you?"

"You are seriously out of touch," Allie told Sam. "I'll believe you have a date with Pres when I see it with my own eyes. Come on, Becky."

Because the twins couldn't get out of it, they left with their dad at seven to go meet his new girlfriend, Stephanie Kramer. Sam helped them get ready, and had to practically wrestle them into fairly conservative skirts and matching cotton sweaters. It was worth it, though, when Sam saw the look on Mr. Jacobs's face. He beamed at his pretty daughters and shot Sam a look of abiding gratitude. Becky and

Allie, meanwhile, acted as if they were being dragged off to prison.

Dressed in faded jeans ripped at the knees, a sexy white lace camisole, a navy blazer, and her red cowboy boots, Sam was just putting the finishing touches on her makeup when the phone rang.

"Babe? It's the Flashman."

"Oh, hi, Flash," Sam said.

"Your shots are ready, and the contact sheet is burning my fingers, it's so hot."

"Really?" Sam asked. "I really did okay?"

"Fantabulous, babe. I kid you not. How about you come by the studio tonight for a little look-see?"

"Oh, gee, I'd love to, but I'm going out," Sam said. "I . . . I've got a date."

Flash said nothing, but Sam could hear a little tapping sound. She guessed he was drumming his fingers on the receiver. Waiting. For what?

"Hey, I know! My friends are picking me up in a few minutes. How about if I stop by there with them? I'm sure they'd love to see the shots."

"No can do, babe," Flash said. "You think having your little friends here while we make vital decisions about your photos is professional behavior?"

"No, I guess not. I mean—" Sam stammered.

"So how's about you lose the buddies early, and you come by the studio after your date? I'll be waiting with some fine bubbly so we can celebrate. If you're really nice"—Flash lowered his voice—"I might even take some more shots of you."

"I . . . I can't," Sam said.

Flash sighed. "Well, frankly, I'm disappointed in you, babe. I thought your professional modeling career was more important to you than some teen-dream date."

"Oh, it is!" Sam assured him, "but—"

"No buts about it, babe. Either you got your priorities straight, or you don't."

"I do, really!" Sam assured him. "How about if I come by tomorrow?"

"Don't know if I could fit you in, babe. I'm busy with girls who take their careers seriously," Flash said coldly.

"Tomorrow night?" Sam said hopefully. "We could look at the shots, and I could pose for you again," she continued in a rush. "I've got tomorrow night off, after nine anyway, and I could see if Emma and Carrie could come—"

"Time out, time out," Flash interrupted. "We know each other now, right?"

"A little," Sam hedged.

"So let me ask you, don't you trust me enough to pose without the protection posse with you?" Flash asked softly.

"Oh, of course I do, but—"

"Okay, so we'll do more shots tomorrow night, nine-thirty," Flash decided. "Belinda and Leonard will be there, if that makes you feel better, babe, but I am not a babysitting service. You come alone."

"Sure," Sam said, trying to sound casual. "No problem. What clothes should I bring this time?"

"I got some stuff here I think would look dynamite on you, so just bring your sweet body. Ciao, babe."

Sam sat on the bed, staring into space. A little voice inside her head said, *Sam, get a grip. You are pleading with a guy who refers to himself as the Flashman.* Then her stomach got into the act, with a queasy, icky feeling. In fact, her entire self was singing the same anxious tune: *Sam, you should not go to this guy's studio alone.*

"Right," she said out loud. "I'll just call him and tell him." *If he's really a professional about this, he won't have any objections*, she told herself as she searched for his business card in the mess on her dresser.

She got as far as dialing the phone number on the card, but she put the phone down before Flash could answer. He'd think she was acting like a child. He's be disgusted. Maybe he'd even stop working with her. And besides, Belinda and Leonard would be there, so she wouldn't actually be alone with him. So what was there to be freaked about?

The doorbell rang downstairs, startling Sam out of her reverie. She fluffed up her hair and ran downstairs.

"Hi," said Pres with an easy grin. "You're lookin' fine," he added appreciatively.

Sam took in his tight, faded jeans and the way his muscles filled out his blue workshirt. "You're looking fine yourself," she said with a smile.

"So, you ready to go? Everybody's in the van. Kurt suggested we head over to Dune Park to check the sunset, then maybe we'll catch some music later."

"Great!" Sam agreed. She climbed into the back of the van with her friends. "*Qué pasa*, vixens?"

"Imagine, so attractive and bilingual, too,"

Carrie quipped from her seat in the front next to Billy.

Kurt was in the backseat with his arm around Emma. Pres climbed in behind Sam. In the very back of the van was a mattress covered with an Indian-print blanket.

"I see this is a real home away from home," Sam said wryly as she sat down on the mattress. "What do you call it, the lust wagon?"

Billy and Pres laughed. "Sorry to disappoint you," Pres said, "but the mattress is to protect our equipment when we're goin' to and from gigs."

Sam looked at Emma and Carrie. "You buy that story?"

"Of course," Carrie said with a serious expression. "These boys are recent arrivals from a monastery."

"A strict one," Emma added.

They arrived at Dune Park just as the sun was beginning to set. After taking a walk down the beach, they took the blanket off the mattress in the back of the van and spread it out on the sand. Fortunately it was oversized, and all six of them were able to sprawl on it comfortably.

"Tell me this island isn't great," Kurt said finally as they watched some gulls soaring overhead.

"You actually grew up here?" Sam asked Kurt.

"Yeah," Kurt said. "My great-grandparents settled here. Growing up on this island makes it hard to suffer from wanderlust. Who would want to leave?"

"I don't know," Sam mused. "I have a feeling I'd suffer from wanderlust no matter where I'd grown up," she said, staring up at the clear sky. "It's amazing to think this is the same sky I stared at in Kansas, but that everything else is totally changed."

No one answered her. Emma was busy kissing Kurt. Billy was nuzzling Carrie's neck, and Pres was just grinning at her in his lazy way.

"I think a walk is a good idea," Pres said, helping Sam up from the blanket.

Hand in hand they headed slowly down the beach, stopping occasionally to skip shells and flat stones out into the ocean.

"So tell me, how did you ever end up on Sunset Island?" Sam asked Pres.

"I studied music for a couple of years at Vanderbilt University in Nashville," Pres said. "My folks were all hot on me bein' a classical musician—you know, symphony orchestras and all that. I was playin' backup for Chris Seldge at the time. Ever hear of him?"

"Sorry, nope," Sam said.

"Well, he's a middlin' country-rock singer, had a pretty big hit out at the time. Anyway, he was starting to tour to push this single, and he asked me to go on the road. It meant droppin' out of school at the beginning of my junior year, but I said yes in a New York minute. No way did I want to be a classical musician. My parents had a fit—"

"I can imagine," Sam said, thinking what her own parents' reaction would be if she told them she wasn't going to Kansas State in the fall.

"For a while touring with Chris was great," Pres said. "Wine, women, and song—well, in my case it was whiskey," Pres admitted. "Anyway, it got real old real fast. And Chris is a mediocre musician at best. I had no respect for the dude, personally or professionally. So one night we're at this club in Portland, and Billy was opening for us, singing with a band called Juice. The band sucked, but Billy was great. He had a great attitude, he was a killer musician, and his head was straight. He was renting this place on Sunset Island—same place we all live in now. He left Juice, I left Chris, and we started writing tunes together. Then we formed Flirting with Danger, and I guess the rest is history."

"So how long ago was that?" Sam asked.

"Two years. Amazin' things have happened in the last year, like openin' for Graham Perry at that benefit. And Polyphonic is real interested in signin' us."

"Not to mention that girls drop like flies in your path," Sam teased.

Pres laughed and looked at Sam. "I don't see you hittin' the turf."

"I don't want to get my jeans full of sand," Sam said.

"Oh, really?" Pres asked, his eyes twinkling.

"Really."

Pres grabbed Sam by the waist and playfully wrestled her to the sand. He tickled her unmercifully until she screamed and shrieked with laughter.

When he finally stopped they were both breathing heavily, and Pres was lying next to Sam in the sand. The next thing Sam knew, Pres's lips were against hers. Sam, whose lips had been around the block a few times, knew a first-class kisser when she kissed one.

"Whoa!" she said breathlessly when their lips finally unlocked. "Why do I have a feeling you've had a lot of experience at this?"

"Maybe," Pres admitted softly, "but kissin' you put me in mind of a song . . ."

"I know!" Sam giggled. "'U Can't Touch This'!"

"Wrong," Pres said with his slow grin. "I was thinkin' more along the lines of 'Feels Like the First Time.'"

They kissed again, and it did.

FIVE

"What do you mean, you're going over there by yourself?" Emma asked Sam.

It was the next day, and Sam, Carrie, and Emma were at the Sunset Country Club with their charges. All the kids were in the pool, and the girls were taking in the noon sun on chaise longues. Sam had just told her friends about her appointment with Flash for that evening. They both had to work, so Sam said she'd just go alone, no big deal. Inside she heaved a sigh of relief, because she wouldn't have to tell them that Flash had told her to come alone.

Sam sat up and reached for the suntan oil. She wanted to have a golden glow in the new pictures she'd be posing for that evening. "Hey, Em, can you get my back?"

Emma grabbed the oil and started rubbing it

into Sam's already tanned back. "It is too a big deal," Emma insisted. "Tell her, Carrie."

"Emma's right," Carrie said. "I don't think it's a good idea."

"Look, this is a professional thing," Sam said. "If I had a job as a . . . a lawyer or something, and I had an appointment, you wouldn't tell me you had to come along."

"This is hardly the same thing," Emma said drily.

Sam just looked at her. "You sound like your mother, Emma." Sam and Carrie had met Emma's mother when she visited the island to see her much-younger fiancé's exhibit at one of the local art galleries. Emma could not stand her mother.

"You're right," Emma said, horrified, "I did. Sorry. Right sentiment, wrong tone of voice."

"Anyway, I won't be alone with Flash—" Sam began.

"Now there's an odious thought," Carrie said.

"—because Leonard and Belinda will be there," Sam explained.

"Come on!" said Emma. "Leonard is Flash's little sycophant, and Belinda hates you!"

"Thank you very much," Sam said.

"You know what I mean," Emma said. "She's

got some kind of chip on her shoulder. My point is that these people are not your friends."

"Friends or not, Flash is not going to try anything with people around," said Sam. "Anyhow, that's not why he's taking more shots. He really believes in me—"

"I don't know, Sam," Carrie interjected.

"Well, that's obviously more than I can say for my two dear friends!" Sam fumed.

"Sam, we're going to the game room with Brent and Brian to play videos," Becky said. She stood over Sam's chaise longue in a tiny red bikini, silver-framed sunglasses shading her eyes. Allie stood next to her, and behind them lounged Brian and Brent, wearing brightly colored surfer jams.

"Okay," said Sam. "We'll hang out about another half-hour, and then we'll meet you in the snack bar."

"Wow, she spoke to you in an almost civil tone of voice," Carrie observed when the twins had left.

"I try," Sam sighed. "Anyway, they're on their best behavior because they want me to keep my mouth shut about them having dates with Brian and Brent at a party tonight."

"Aren't those guys a little old for the twins?" Emma asked.

"I agree," Sam said. "Brian and Brent are sixteen, and they look it. But Mr. Jacobs has gotten so involved in this new romance of his that he's kind of oblivious to the girls right now. He told them they could go to the party, but he didn't tell them who they could or couldn't go with." She shrugged.

"Do you think maybe you should tell him?" Carrie asked.

"I don't know." Sam sighed. "What I did was, I told them they absolutely had to be home by midnight. I'll be back way before that. I told them that if they get home on time, sober, and fully dressed, I'll keep my mouth shut."

"That's a tough call," Emma said sympathetically. "I'm just glad the Hewitt kids are younger and I don't have to deal with stuff like that."

"Speak of the devil," Carrie said as three-year-old Katie Hewitt and four-year-old Chloe Templeton came toddling over to them holding hands with their beloved swimming teacher, Kurt Ackerman.

"I believe you know these lovely ladies," Kurt said, sitting down on the edge of Emma's lounge chair. Emma smiled at Kurt. God, he was gorgeous.

"Me and Chloe swimmed!" Katie exclaimed to Emma.

"That's great, honey," Emma said, tearing her eyes away from Kurt. She gave Katie a hug.

"I put my face under the water," Chloe told Carrie proudly, cuddling up to her au pair. Exhausted from swimming, Chole and Katie snuggled up to their babysitters and closed their eyes.

Kurt leaned close to Emma. "You look gorgeous," he murmured. "You're wearing my favorite swimsuit. Need some sunblock anywhere? Everywhere?" he asked her hopefully.

"Please! My virgin ears!" Sam protested. She turned over onto her back. "Ahhhh, this is the life," she sighed happily.

"Well, if it isn't my favorite friends," sing-songed Lorell's unmistakable voice.

"Correction: this *was* the life," Sam said, squinting up at Lorell. With Lorell were the ever-present Daphne and Diana. A skimpy bathing suit showed Diana's perfectly aerobi-cized figure off to great advantage, but Daphne looked frighteningly skeletal in her black maillot.

"Notice that they travel in packs, like wolves," Sam observed darkly.

"Is this chaise free?" Lorell asked, plopping herself down next to Sam's chair. "Hey, Kurt," she added, smiling seductively at him.

"Hi," said Kurt easily. Ever since Lorell and Diana had staged the nasty little exhibition that nearly ruined Emma's summer if not her life, they'd delighted in sniping at Kurt whenever they ran into him—especially if he was with Emma. But recently Kurt had shut them up with a clever comeback of his own. Now it seemed that, at least as far as Kurt was concerned, they'd declared some kind of truce. Kurt didn't care particularly one way or the other. He was perfectly happy to be civil to them as long as they did the same.

"Say, Kurt, I was wondering if I could schedule some lessons with you," Diana asked innocently. "I've been wanting to learn to dive."

Kurt looked over at Diana. She had on an aqua bikini that set off her chestnut-colored curls and deep-set blue eyes.

"Sure," said Kurt. "Sign up at the swim desk. I'll see when I can fit you in."

"I have to admit I'm a little afraid of diving," Diana continued, "so I may need a lot of personal attention."

"No prob," Kurt said easily. "Overcoming fear is the first step." He tossed the sunblock into Emma's beachbag and got up from her chaise longue. "Duty calls," he said. "I'll call you later," he added to Emma.

"Aqua Man has some serious buns," Diana said as she watched Kurt walk away.

"And pecs," Lorell added. "Nice pecs."

"I wouldn't mind feeling those hunky arms around me," Diana said. She looked over at Emma innocently. "You two aren't exactly going steady or anything, are you?"

Sam saw the murderous look on Emma's face, and she sat up quickly. "Do you smell something?" she asked, sniffing ostentatiously. "Gee, it really stinks around here. I think we should move."

"I agree," said Emma as she and Carrie grabbed their beachbags and towels.

"Oh, don't leave now!" Lorell pouted. "We wanted to hear all about Sammi's little modeling career with Flash Hathaway!"

"Yeah," Daphne giggled nervously. "Did he talk you out of your clothes yet?"

"Look, this is a completely professional gig," Sam said brusquely, pushing her hair out of her face.

"I'm so sure," Daphne snorted.

"Now, now, Daphne," Lorell rebuked her. "Maybe girls like Sam consider X-rated photos of themselves a positive career move."

Sam was going to put her fist through Lorell's smug face, no doubt about it. Emma and Carrie saw the look on Sam's face, and gently towed her toward the clubhouse. This was somewhat complicated by the fact that Emma and Carrie were each also holding a plump and soundly sleeping pre-schooler.

"Bye!" Carrie called back to them. "Lovely chatting with you!"

"I'm going to kill the bitch, and no jury will find me guilty," Sam growled as soon as they were far enough away not to be overheard.

"You're the one who told us that revenge is more satisfying than murder," Carrie reminded Sam.

"I changed my mind," Sam told her.

They headed for the snack bar, where they had arranged to meet all their charges. They bought Cokes and slices of pizza and settled at a table.

"Seriously, Sam," Emma said, fiddling with her straw, "I'm really concerned about this thing tonight."

"Don't start," Sam warned.

"Well, if you go alone, people will talk. If we're with you, no one can say anything," Emma explained.

Sam put down her slice of pizza and stared at Emma. "People will talk?" she repeated quietly. "Like who? Daphne? Lorell? Diana? You mean snotty rich girls will talk?"

"I just meant—"

"I know what you meant," Sam said, obviously angry.

"She meant she's concerned about you, is all," Carrie explained. "I am, too."

"Look, either you trust me or you don't. Either you believe me or you don't," Sam said.

"It's not you we don't trust! It's him!" Carrie exclaimed.

Sam shook her head. "Why? You think Flash is only in it for what he can get, too? Well, that just isn't true! I happen to have a big future as a model! Everyone says so! Besides, I can take care of myself!" Sam pushed back her chair and stormed off in the direction of the game room to get the twins. Maybe Emma and Carrie meant well, but it was obvious that they just didn't understand.

As the twins waited nervously by the front door for Brent and Brian, Sam had some serious second thoughts about her agreement with them. For once they weren't dressed identically, but it was a tossup as to which sister was dressed more trashily.

Becky wore a skintight, hot-pink stretch dress that barely covered her butt, over black lace-textured pantyhose worn with strappy black spike heels. Allie had on the shortest of fire-engine-red miniskirts with a microscopic black halter top; matching red suspenders framed her alarmingly pointed breasts. Both girls had managed to inflate their hair to about twice its normal size, and had obviously been just as enthusiastic with their makeup. They looked like something out of an X-rated vampire movie.

Sam sighed. "You guys, remember your promise," she reminded them again.

"Yeah, yeah, we know," Becky muttered.

Mr. Jacobs came in from the den. He raised his eyebrows when he saw what his daughters were wearing to the party.

"Aren't your clothes a little . . . snug?" he asked them.

"Dad, this is how *all* the girls at the party will be dressed," Allie huffed, rolling her eyes. "It's the style."

"Yeah, Dad, this is what *everyone* wears," Becky added.

Mr. Jacobs smiled uncertainly. "I guess I'm a little out of touch," he acknowledged.

A midnight-blue Porsche pulled into the Jacobses' driveway, tires squealing. "Who's driving?" Mr. Jacobs asked with a frown.

"Oh, the older brother of one of our friends,"

Allie said quickly. "Bye, dad." She kissed him on the cheek, as did her sister, and they ran out to the car.

"All the girls really dress like that?" Mr. Jacobs asked Sam, smiling in his worried way.

"Really," Sam said. "They're okay," she assured him. And she fervently hoped that she was telling the truth.

This time around, Sam blew into Flash's studio like a pro. She came with freshly washed hair devoid of spray or gel, her face scrubbed free of makeup.

"Right on time, babe. I like that," Flash said, giving Sam a hug. His hands wandered down past her hips and she stepped back quickly.

"So, where are the shots? Can I see them?" Sam asked.

"Sure, but I want to get a couple of rolls in tonight, so we gotta get started. After that we'll sit down, chill out, and look at your contact sheets, okay?" Flash was running his hand down Sam's arm. It felt creepy.

"Sure," said Sam, plastering a smile on her face. "Uh, where's Belinda? I guess I should get made up."

"We're all alone," Flash said in a low voice.

Sam's heart pounded in her chest. She took a step backward. "But . . . I thought . . ."

"Come on, let's get going. I haven't got all night," said a cold female voice. Sam spun around and looked into the sour face of Belinda.

Sam looked back at Flash, who now wore a smug grin. "But I thought you said—"

"Just a joke, babe," Flash said easily. "You are one scared little chicken."

"She's not a *chicken*," Belinda said sharply.

"Whoa, sisterhood is powerful," Flash observed sarcastically.

"Come on," said Belinda, turning on her heel and striding toward the makeup room.

"So, how long have you been working for Flash?" Sam asked as Belinda began to apply the makeup base.

"Too long," Belinda said. "Close your eyes." Sam obliged and Belinda patted the base onto Sam's eyelids.

"You don't seem real happy here," Sam observed.

"Well, aren't you the rocket scientist," Belinda said, reaching for an eyebrow pencil.

"Look, I'm just trying to be friendly," Sam said. "There's no need to bite my head off. If you hate your job so much, who don't you quit instead of taking it out on me?"

Belinda pressed her lips together and slowly wiped a tissue over the tip of the eyebrow pencil. "Sorry," she said finally. "I do need to find a new job."

"I think being a makeup artist sounds like great fun," Sam said.

Belinda gave a short, bitter laugh. "It sucks," she said, feathering in Sam's eyebrows. "But I dropped out of school to model. I'm not exactly trained for anything."

Sam was shocked. Belinda? A model? Sam looked more closely at Belinda's angry, pinched face. *Why, she's actually very pretty*, Sam realized. *It's just that her permanent scowl keeps a person from noticing anything else*.

"So what happened?" Sam asked, fascinated.

"What happened is that it didn't work out, obviously," Belinda said. "Close your eyes." She brushed a coppery shadow across Sam's eyelids. "I was a jerk. I believed I was going to be this big, successful model. I'm the prettiest girl in Altoona, Michigan—or at least I was," Belinda said bitterly. "I sent my pictures to this New York modeling agency. They called me in Altoona and told me I had potential, that I should come to New York and have a portfolio done. So I came on Christmas vacation my senior year. Well, it turned out this modeling agency was going to charge me for the portfolio—eight hundred dollars. It was all the money I had. I gave it to them, and I got pictures, and then nothing happened. That agency never got me any work. And everyplace else I took the pictures to told me they weren't even professional-quality shots. I didn't even have enough money to get back to Altoona. Then I met a real professional photographer, and he said he'd redo the shots for free because I had so much potential, and he did. Not only did he save my butt, but I fell for him in a big way."

"Flash Hathaway?" Sam asked, totally fascinated.

Belinda laughed again. "His real name is Fred Hathwonowski, but don't tell him I told you so. Anyway, when he got an offer to work for Universal Models out of their Portland office, I came with him. He dropped me— personally and professionally—and here I am. Now I just work for the jerk. Blot your lips."

Sam blotted her lipstick on the tissue Belinda handed her. "Why don't you go home?" Sam asked her.

"To Altoona?" Belinda asked, looking at Sam as if she were crazy.

God, this sounds too much like me, was

Sam's horrified thought. "Listen, Belinda, does Flash—Fred—does he only test girls to, well, to try and get into their pants?"

"Sometimes," Belinda admitted. "And sometimes he truly thinks the girl can make it, and sometimes it's both. Close your eyes so I can powder you down," Belinda instructed.

"And with me?" Sam asked in a little voice.

"That you'll have to find out for yourself," Belinda said as she dabbed on the loose powder. "I can tell you this, though: sleazy as he is, he's one hell of a good photographer. Come on, I'll show you what you're supposed to wear," Belinda said, leading her into the dressing room.

Hanging on hooks were two outfits. The first one was a diaphanous black lace nightgown, with a black lace teddy that went underneath. The second was a skimpy, see-through leopard-print bustier with a matching leopard-print string bikini.

Sam looked at Belinda. "You're kidding," Sam said.

Belinda shrugged. "Lingerie models make a fortune. It pays double the regular catalogue rate."

"Really?" Sam asked dubiously.

"Lots of big models do it. Harlow McPhee just did a lingerie spread in *Vogue* this month."

Belinda said, naming one of the top models in the world.

Belinda left and Sam stared at the outfits.

"Hurry up, babe," Flash called in to her. "My creative juices are flowing!"

Sam nervously unbuttoned her shirt and stepped out of her shorts. The black negligee seemed the more modest of the two outfits, so she hurriedly put it on. To her dismay, she could faintly see the outline of her breasts through the thin material of the teddy and the gown.

The curtain opened abruptly. "Fantabulous, babe!" Flash said, staring at Sam. "Let's get you under the lights."

Sam took a deep breath and smiled at Flash, who led her out of the dressing room.

"You make my heart stop in that outfit, babe," Flash said, looking at her through his camera.

"I feel a little, um, bare," Sam said tentatively.

"Hey, you want to act like a pro or you want to act like a kid?" Flash said with a look of disgust on his face. Sam looked around the room at the various photo spreads that adorned the walls. She saw photos of models she recognized in string bikinis, in wet, see-through shirts with nothing underneath, even topless. Well, if they could do it, she could do it.

"A pro," Sam said, straightening her shoulders and shaking her head so that her hair rippled across her shoulders.

Flash grinned. "Now you're talking! Leonard, crank up the tunes!" From wherever Leonard was he turned on the sound system. "It's magic time!" Flash yelled.

Sam's self-consciousness left her quickly. She twirled and posed, pouting her lips, putting her hands low on her hips, looking over her shoulder seductively. Flash's shouts of encouragement egged her on. It didn't feel sleazy at all; it felt fabulous.

"You pose like you been doin' it forever!" Flash exclaimed. "These will be dynamite. Let's do the next outfit."

Sam ran back into the dressing room and took off the black outfit. She slipped on the leopard-print string bikini bottoms first. Just as she was reaching for the bustier, Flash opened the curtain. Sam immediately covered her breasts with her arms.

"No, thanks," Sam managed, still keeping her arms folded across her chest. "I can do it fine myself."

Flash just stood there, looking at her.

Is he waiting for me to change? Sam thought frantically. *In front of him?*

"Well, hurry up," Flash finally told her, still staring at her.

"I . . . uh . . . I feel a little uncomfortable changing with you here," she told him honestly. "As soon as you leave, I'll be ready in a second."

Flash curled his upper lip. "Hey, babe, let me ask you something," he sneered. "You think your bare boobs are such a big deal?"

Sam had never felt so mortified. "Uh, no, that's not it, it's just that—"

"You better wise up, babe. What do you think goes on backstage at a fashion show? The girls are running around half naked, getting zipped and sewn into the outfits. You think they think twice about some photographer seeing everything they got? You think they stand there squealing, 'Oh, no! I can't change until there are no men around'? Because I'll tell you, babe, they'd be out of work real fast."

"It's just that you startled me," Sam said. She turned away from him and grabbed the bustier quickly. Flash came up behind her. She could feel him breathing on her neck.

"I'll help you hook it," he said in a low voice. "Belinda had to leave."

Sam held the front of the bustier in place with shaking hands while Flash did up the hooks in back.

"I'm gonna put the fan on you for this one," Flash said, "so your hair will blow. We'll get the Sheena, Queen of the Jungle look."

"Sounds cool," Sam managed. She continued to adjust the front of the bustier so that she wouldn't have to turn around and face Flash, and she heaved a sigh of relief when he left the dressing room. She stared at herself in the mirror. The entire bustier was see-through. Her breasts could be seen quite clearly, nipples and all.

Okay, so your boobs show, so what? Sam told herself. *You're not in Junction, Kansas, anymore. After all, if you're going to be self-conscious about your body, you shouldn't be a model.*

Sam took a deep breath and walked out of the dressing room, stepping under the hot lights. Flash had aimed a fan at her, which blew her hair back—and made her nipples harden instantly.

"Yeah! Now we're talking!" Flash bellowed, aiming his camera at Sam. "Lick your lips, babe. Show me how hot you can be."

Sam thought about all the times she's posed,

all alone, in front of the mirror in her bedroom. She thought about how she had dreamed about just the opportunity she was getting at that very minute. *I will not blow this*, she vowed. She pretended Flash was Presley, and then she felt confident again. She felt sexy, too, imagining Pres there admiring her brazenness. When she got into that fantasy, she sort of had fun.

"These shots will be even better than the first set," Flash predicted. "I'm telling you, you're a natural."

Maybe it was really true! *Okay, so he saw my boobs—the rest of it wasn't so bad*, Sam told herself as she quickly changed back into her shorts and shirt. Flash didn't come in, which made her feel better. In fact, by the time Sam joined Flash in his office to look at the contact sheets from their first photo session, she was feeling pretty good about everything.

Flash sat on the couch and patted the seat next to him.

"Take a look-see," he said.

Sam took the loupe from Flash and leaned forward to examine the four contact sheets that were spread on the coffee table. On the contact sheet the photos were tiny, about one inch by one inch, but the loupe magnified them, giving Sam a sense of how they would look when they were printed.

"Is this really me?" Sam asked. "I look . . . these are . . . you're a genius!" she exclaimed.

"Hey, I had a great model, babe," Flash said. "I told you, you are a natural."

Sam hardly noticed Flash's hand rubbing her back as she eagerly leaned forward to examine her shots. "You'll help me pick the right ones to blow up?" she asked him.

"Put yourself in my hands, babe. After all, the Flashman hasn't let you down yet, has he?"

"No, you really haven't," Sam agreed.

Flash leaned forward with her, his hand casually draped across her thigh. She could feel him breathing in her ear, and his hand started up the leg of her baggy shorts.

"I brought coffee," Belinda called out loudly, banging the office door open. She set a paper bag on Flash's desk.

"Gee, thanks," Flash said sarcastically.

Sam shot Belinda a grateful look.

"I'm going to go straighten up the makeup room," Belinda said. "I hope you're not going to be too long, Sam." She turned to Flash. "I promised Sam a ride home. She took the trolley into town." Sam pretended she was busy looking at one of the contact sheets. It was true she had taken the trolley over, but she had never had any such conversation with Belinda.

Flash looked disgusted. He handed Sam the contact sheets. "Here. I got another set. Look 'em over at home. I got things to do, babe. I'll call ya."

Sam found Belinda and they made their way out to Belinda's car. "This was a really nice thing you did for me," Sam said as Belinda backed out of her parking space.

"I didn't do it for you," Belinda said shortly.

"You're still hung up on him?" Sam asked.

Belinda didn't answer, and finally Sam just gave her directions to the Jacobses' house.

"Thanks again," Sam said, getting out of the car. "You were right, by the way. He's a terrific photographer."

"Yeah," Belinda said with a short laugh. "If only he were a terrific human being."

SIX

The following morning the twins were scheduled for their second rehearsal for the fashion show, and as usual they were running late.

"Hey, hurry it up, you guys!" Sam yelled down the hall for the fifth time. "You're supposed to be there in fifteen minutes!" She sighed and marched down the hall yet again to pester them. She wasn't in the best of moods. She had woken up with a feeling of anxiety in her stomach about the outfits she had posed in the night before. The bottom line was, she was embarrassed. No way could she tell her friends that she'd posed for Flash in such revealing lingerie.

She yanked the quilt up on her bed, which still left the room a total mess. On the theory that what didn't show didn't count, Sam kicked her clothes into the bottom of her closet. "Okay, so neatness isn't my long suit," she said out loud, retrieving a stray high heel from the center of the floor and throwing it under her bed.

Sam grabbed her purse and headed down the hall to get the twins. She heard them arguing as she approached their room.

"I'm telling you, Brent won't give it back!" Allie yelled.

"Oh yeah? That Brian's the sleaze. It was his idea!" Becky screamed back at her sister.

"What was his idea?" Sam asked when she reached their doorway.

"Nothing," Allie said sullenly.

"Did something happen at the party last night?" Sam asked.

"Like she said, nothing," Becky mumbled. Her eyes wouldn't meet Sam's.

Sam knew something was up but she didn't have time to cross-examine them. "Come on, we'll talk about it later."

The three of them climbed into the Jacobses' Subaru and Sam backed the car down the driveway. "You know, when you make a professional commitment, like being in a fashion show, you have to act professionally," Sam told them as she drove toward the Sunset Inn, where the rehearsal was taking place. "That means being on time."

"Thanks for the advice, Mom," Becky said sarcastically.

"I don't know why I even bother," Sam muttered under her breath as she parked the car.

"Jeez, you don't need to come in with us," Allie said as Sam was getting out of the car. "You came to the first rehearsal. Wasn't that bad enough?"

"Watching over your angelic selves is my sole pleasure in life," Sam said drily. "Besides, I promised your dad I'd stay."

The twins sighed tragically and walked into the inn ahead of Sam.

"You're late," Pamela Winslow said in a no-nonsense voice when she saw the twins. She checked her clipboard for information. "You're supposed to be trying on the junior casual outfits from Savannah's this morning." Pamela pointed to the far left corner of the giant room, and the girls quickly scooted off in that direction.

"Sorry they were late," Sam told Pamela. "I did everything but light a fire under them."

Pamela smiled wearily. "This is just not my day. Two of my models took off for Hawaii; the girl who was supposed to model the bridal gown at the end of the show broke her ankle; and the show is Saturday."

"Well, today is Sunday," Sam said. "That still gives you almost a week to replace her."

"I wish it were that easy," Pam said. "The gown was made especially to fit her, because it's the actual gown her parents are purchasing for her wedding in six months. So you see, we can't alter it to fit another model."

"Well, make it like Cinderella," Sam giggled. "You know, search for a model who has her measurements and can fit into the gown!"

"It's a little tough." Pam sighed. "Kimmy— that's the model—is almost six feet tall and very slender. It's hard to find a—" Pam stopped talking and her eyes lit up. "You!" she said, pointing at Sam.

"Me?" Sam said.

"I don't have any girls in the show who would fit into Kimmy's gown, but I bet you would fit into it beautifully!"

"I told you," Sam said, "I really can't—"

"Oh, why not?" Pam implored her.

"I just did my second photo shoot for Universal Models," Sam explained. "I have my professional career to think about. . . ."

"Don't you think other professional models

started out in amateur fashion shows?" Pam asked gently.

"Maybe," Sam said, "but they did it before they were professionals." What Sam was thinking, but didn't add, was that she couldn't possibly be in the same show the twins were in. It would be too humiliating. After all, they already looked up to her as a real model.

"Well, if you change your mind, will you call me? The finale of the show is all wedding fashions, and it was all built around this spectacular gown. No model, no gown. No gown, no big finale," Pam sighed.

"Don't count on it," Sam said with a shrug. "Sorry."

Sam sat out of the way and read a book until the twins were finished. They were unusually subdued on the ride home.

"Are you two okay?" Sam asked them.

"Fine," said Allie, staring out the window.

"Did something happen at the party last night you want to talk about?" Sam pressed. She knew something was wrong.

"Nothing happened," Allie snapped.

"And we don't want to talk about it," Becky added.

"Well, if you ever do want to talk—" Sam began.

"We don't!" Becky yelled. "So just butt out!"

"And people wonder why I call you monsters," Sam said sweetly as she turned the corner onto their street.

A motorcycle was in their driveway, with a tall, muscular guy leaning against it, helmet in hand.

The twins pushed the buttons to lower their windows and stuck their heads out. "Oh my God, it's Presley!" Becky screamed.

Well, well, thought Sam. *What a nice surprise.* She wished she had put on something cuter than her old white cotton shorts and a pink-and-white striped tank top that had seen better days.

"Don't tell him we're thirteen, I'm begging you," Allie implored.

"One minute it's 'butt out,' the next minute it's 'let's be pals,'" Sam noted ironically as she pulled into the driveway.

"We'll never say anything mean again," Becky promised. "Just don't tell him."

Sam cut the ignition and turned to face the twins. "You know, there's nothing wrong with being thirteen, you guys! Thirteen is—"

But Becky and Allie were already scrambling out of the car, running over to their idol.

"We love your music!" Becky gushed to

Pres. "We heard you at the Play Café twice, and in the park last summer at that outdoor concert!"

"It was awesome!" Allie added.

"Thanks," said Pres easily, but he was looking over their heads at Sam, who was strolling toward him. "Watchin' you walk brightens my day," he said, grinning at her.

"I'll take that as a compliment," Sam said. "Nice to see you, too."

"What's Billy like?" Allie asked Pres eagerly. "He is totally gorgeous."

"He's not really dating some friend of Sam's, is he?" Becky asked.

"Girls, you cut me to the quick," Pres said, his hand over his heart. "Here I thought you were *my* number-one fans."

"Oh, we are!" Becky assured him, Allie nodding her agreement. "I said you were cutest, but Allie said Billy was."

"I did not!" Allie screamed. "You can be such a little—"

"Did you even introduce yourself before you started fighting?" Sam asked the twins.

"Are you coming in?" Becky asked Pres, completely ignoring Sam. "Wait till I tell my friend Darcy you were here. She'll never believe me. Can you just stand here long enough for me to call Darcy?"

"Not this time, but I'll catch you again, an' that's a promise," Pres drawled. He handed Sam a second helmet from the back of his bike. "You up for a ride?"

"Absolutely," Sam told him. She turned to the twins. "Tell your dad I'll be back in fifteen minutes or so," she said, then started to climb on the back of the bike.

"Nice meetin' you, girls," Pres said politely as he helped Sam get on the back of his bike. She slid her arms around his waist. "Well now, doesn't that feel good," Pres said with a small grin as he started up the bike.

The girls were still standing in the driveway staring after them as Pres and Sam roared away on the bike.

"I didn't know you owned a motorcycle," Sam yelled over the sound of the wind rushing by them.

"I don't," Pres said. "I borrowed it from Wheels for the afternoon." Wheels was a bike and motorbike rental shop on the boardwalk where Pres worked part-time. He turned down a side road, then another, and finally they ended up at a secluded beach way off the beaten path.

"Kurt told me about this spot," Pres said as they got off the bike. "He made me promise not to go around tellin' people where it is."

100

"I see why," Sam said, looking over the stretch of beach that ended in clear blue ocean. They sat down in the sand, enjoying the solitude. Sam could see a huge yacht in the distance. "I'd like to go on a cruise someday," Sam sighed.

"Where to?" Pres asked, leaning back on his elbows.

"Oh, I don't know." Sam shrugged. "Almost anywhere. Mesopotamia. Timbuktu. Ohio. I just want to see the whole world."

"Yeah, that's how I feel, too," Pres said. "I guess that's one of the reasons it was so attractive to me when Chris asked me to tour with him. I thought, wow, someone's actually gonna pay me to play music and travel, my two favorite things in the world? Dang!"

"Dang?" Sam repeated, looking at Pres with a teasing grin. "You Southern boys are so quaint." Presley kissed her. "You kiss great, too, I might add."

"Aw, shucks, ma'am, it's nothin'," he said.

"Oh, it's something, all right," Sam said. "Is it something in the water down there in Tennessee? Because I don't recall any of the guys in Kansas kissing like this."

"Hmm, just how many of the guys in Kansas have you kissed, anyway?" Pres asked.

"A lot," Sam said truthfully.

Presley laughed heartily and kissed her again.

"I have to get back soon," Sam said, pulling away from him regretfully.

"Well, actually, I came by to ask you somethin'," Pres said. "The Flirts have a gig this coming weekend at the Jelloman's in Bangor. I thought you might like to come."

"I've heard of the Jelloman's!" Sam exclaimed. "The owner is a real heavyset guy— he's in all their ads in the paper. Every weekend the club features jello wrestling, right? Female customers get in a ring full of jello?"

"Yeah," Pres admitted.

"Is it, like, some obnoxious, sexist thing? You know, some new twist on wet T-shirt contests or something?"

Presley shrugged. "It makes no never mind to me. We're goin' there to play, the pay is great, end of story."

"Well, what night is it?" Sam asked. "I usually have one of the weekend nights off."

"It's the whole weekend. We're stayin' in a real nice hotel near the club."

Sam pushed her red curls out of her face. "You're inviting me away for the weekend?" she asked slowly.

"Yep."

"Is this, like, a one-room, one-bed kind of an invitation?" Sam asked.

"I got to hand it to you, girl, you do get down to brass tacks," Pres acknowledged.

"Meaning the answer is yes," Sam said.

"Would that be bad?" Pres asked her carelessly.

"Not necessarily," she said. "I just need to think about it." She got up and brushed off her shorts. "I really do have to get back."

When they reached the Jacobses' house, Sam got off the bike and handed Presley his helmet.

"Fun ride?" Pres asked Sam.

"Fun," she agreed.

He kissed her cheek, then he kissed the edge of her mouth, then he kissed her full on the lips. "So you'll let me know?" Pres asked softly.

"I'll let you know."

Pres kissed her again, put on his helmet, and roared away on the motorcycle.

"Oh my God, he was kissing you!" Becky screamed when Sam came in the front door.

"We couldn't tell if he French-kissed you from this angle," Allie said. "Did he?"

"Did you two have your faces pressed against the window?" Sam asked them.

103

"Of course," Becky answered seriously. "So, did he?"

"None of your business. What do you guys want for lunch?" Sam asked, walking into the kitchen.

"How can you talk about food at a time like this?" Becky demanded.

"Like what?" Sam asked. "Besides, I'm hungry, even if you're not."

"We can't eat lunch anymore," Allie said. "The outfits from Savannah's were a little tight, and we both need to lose five pounds."

"Who said?" Sam asked, her hands on her hips.

"No one said, exactly," Becky explained, "but it's, like, so obvious. And that girl you were talking to at the audition, Daphne whatever, she's modeling right after us and we look like cows next to her."

"They hired Daphne to model?" Sam asked, completely surprised.

"Oh, the woman who owns Savannah's is her aunt or something," Becky said. "Anyway, I was looking at myself in the mirror when I was standing next to her, and my thighs are twice as big as hers!"

"Listen, something is wrong with Daphne," Sam said, pulling out a loaf of bread. "I think she's got a lot of problems, and she's way too thin. How does a tunafish sandwich sound?" she said, reaching for the can.

"Sure, you can eat tuna with gobs of mayo, you're naturally thin," Becky complained, "but we can't. Even Brian and Brent said we were getting fat."

"Yeah, they said only really skinny girls should wear their skirts as short as we do," Allie added.

"They did not," Sam said, getting the mayonnaise from the fridge.

"God, you're just as bad as Dad!" Becky exclaimed. "Don't you ever listen?"

Sam stopped with her spoon halfway into the mayonnaise. "Okay, you're right. I wasn't there. I didn't hear the conversation. I'm sorry. Anyway, you should decide about your looks and your weight on your own, not based on some guy's opinion," she concluded.

"Oh yeah, like you don't." Allie snorted. "If Flash told you you had to lose weight or gain weight or wear certain clothes to be a model, wouldn't you do it?"

"That's a professional thing," Sam argued. "It's different."

"You're totally hypocritical!" Allie said with disgust. "You might as well be an adult! Come on, Becky, let's go call our boyfriends."

Sam stared at the tunafish, but she was thinking about what Allie had said about her being a hypocrite. "That can't be me," Sam whispered to herself. She had always prided herself on her honesty, and Allie's words hurt. An image of herself in the sleazy leopard-print bustier popped into her mind. "Lick your lips, stick out your boobs," Flash had said, and she had done everything he asked.

Suddenly she wasn't so hungry anymore.

SEVEN

The next morning Sam sat at the breakfast table leisurely sipping her second cup of coffee. Mercifully, the twins had already left to go on some marathon bike ride with their friends, and Sam had the entire day off. She was planning to meet Emma and Carrie on the boardwalk at ten.

"Sam, could I talk with you a minute?" Mr. Jacobs said, coming into the kitchen.

"Sure," said Sam.

Mr. Jacobs sat down and ran his hand through his thinning hair. "I know this is your day off. I just wanted to ask your opinion about something."

He hesitated, and Sam nodded her encouragement.

"Well, you're so good with the twins," he continued earnestly, "I thought maybe you could help me out on this. Stephanie Kramer and I are getting kind of serious . . . you know I took the girls out to dinner with us the other night so we could all start to get to know one another better. It was the first time Stephanie had met the twins. Well, they were pretty awful to her. I think she's still in a state of shock. I'm sure the girls were just feeling awkward and that's why they behaved that way. I want Stephanie to see how sweet and loving Becky and Allie really are, and I'm not sure how to handle it."

Sam practically choked on her coffee. Becky and Allie, sweet and loving? "Gee, Mr. Jacobs, I'm not sure . . ." she hedged.

"I was wondering if maybe you could talk to them," Mr. Jacobs asked hopefully. "The girls really look up to you."

"They do?" Sam asked.

"Absolutely!" Mr. Jacobs affirmed. "They talk about you all the time. Everything is Sam this and Sam that. You're a real role model for them."

"I'm not exactly sure what you want me to say to them," Sam said.

"Just . . . oh, something about how you know that even if I decided to marry again, I wouldn't love them any less, that our family could be even better, things like that," Mr. Jacobs explained. "That Stephanie's interested in getting to know them better, if they'll just give her a chance."

"I'll try," Sam said, "but don't you think it would be better if you talked with them yourself?"

"I'm not very good at that, as I guess you've noticed," Mr. Jacobs said with a sheepish grin. "And you've been so good for the girls already," he continued. "They're really starting to act like young ladies, thanks to you."

Mr. Jacobs wandered back into his den and Sam sat at the table shaking her head. Unbelievable. He certainly had a different opinion of the twins than she did. He must be living in a whole different reality, in fact.

After a quick shower, Sam threw on a pair of baggy men's boxer shorts covered with peace signs, and an oversized man's white T-shirt, loosely tucked in. She cinched the shorts with a belt below the elastic waistband, added sneakers and sunglasses, and headed out the door.

Emma and Carrie were already at the pier when Sam arrived.

"Ah, she makes her entrance," Carrie said when she saw Sam.

Emma looked at Sam's outfit. "I love the way you put clothes together. It amazes me."

Sam looked down at herself. "This? What's the big deal?"

"I just would never even think of wearing men's boxer shorts and a T-shirt," Emma said admiringly.

"I might think of it, but I'd never do it," said Carrie. She had on denim overalls, unhooked on one side, over a white cotton T-shirt.

"Why not?" Sam asked. "It would look cute on you."

"I don't know." Carrie shrugged. "Adventure in fashion is not my forte. Besides, everything looks great on you. I'd feel like my hips looked a mile wide in those boxer shorts."

Sam sat next to Carrie on a bench and held her face up to the morning sun. "This body-image thing of yours has got to go," Sam counseled. "You do not have big hips." She jumped up and pulled Carrie and Emma off the bench. "Come on, let's go find some junk food."

"She's impossible," Carrie groaned to Emma.

The three girls walked slowly along the boardwalk, chewing happily on a bag of salt-water taffy that Sam had bought.

"Mmmm, sugar before noon, don't you love

it?" Sam asked, reaching for another piece of taffy. "What should we do today?"

"Before we decide that I want to hear all about your photo session with Flash on Saturday," Carrie said.

"We were really concerned about you," Emma added.

"It was a piece of cake, just like I told you it would be," Sam said. "I posed, he took pictures, end of story."

"Really?" Carrie asked. "He didn't try anything?"

"Nothing I couldn't handle," Sam said nonchalantly, licking some taffy off one finger.

"What do you mean, nothing you couldn't handle?" Emma asked, concerned. "He did try something?"

"No, of course not!" Sam told her. "He's a professional. It was just an expression. Get over it, will you?"

"Well, I'm glad to hear he didn't put any moves on you," Carrie said firmly. "Just be careful he doesn't, that's all."

"I wish you guys would stop treating me like a baby!" Sam said exasperatedly. "Did it ever occur to you that I came here for a little freedom from small-town thinking? You know, I already have parents, in case you were wondering. I can call them up any time I want to hear this kind of stuff." The truth was that Sam felt guilty—about the sexy shoot and about sort of lying to her friends. Sam hated to feel guilty about anything.

"Sam, I'm sorry," Emma said contritely. "It's just that we're your friends and we care about you." She wanted to somehow make it up to Sam, so she decided to avoid talking about the odious Flash and concentrate instead on Sam's modeling career. "So, what did you wear this time?"

"Oh, different stuff," Sam said evasively. God! What a bunch of busybodies! Couldn't they just leave her alone about this?

Emma bit her lip.

"Like what?" Carrie pursued.

"You know, things he thought would look good on me, to see how I shoot best," Sam said. "Like last time. Hey, want to rent some bikes?"

"What kind of things did he think would look good, Sam?" Carrie wanted to know. "There's something you're not telling us," she added, staring at Sam.

"What is this, true confessions?" Sam said. Her friends just stared at her. "Okay, some lingerie," Sam mumbled.

"Oh, no!" Emma cried. "Were the shots . . . decent?"

"Please, Emma, don't go into your proper-little-rich-girl routine on me," Sam said with disgust. "It was no big deal. Professional models do lingerie layouts all the time!"

"Was it sleazy?" Carrie asked.

"No, the shots were not sleazy. The lingerie was beautiful, very classy stuff. I show more on the beach every day, for your information," Sam said hotly. She threw the taffy into the nearest trash bin and pulled on her sunglasses angrily.

"As long as you're sure," Emma said quietly. She was still stinging from Sam's rich-girl remark.

"I'm sure," Sam said. She was very eager to change the subject. "Hey, guess who came over yesterday?"

Carrie and Emma exchanged a look. They both felt that Sam was hiding something from them, but they also knew that they'd pushed her as far as they could.

"Wipe those worrywart looks off your faces," Sam demanded. "I'm trying to tell you something important! Pres came over! On a motorcycle! The twins were dying of envy."

"They know Flirting with Danger?" Emma asked, surprised.

113

"I didn't realize how popular they are myself," Sam said. "You would have thought some movie star was standing in our driveway."

"I bet Pres loved that," Carrie said with a grin.

"He was very nice to them," Sam said. "The other day I told the twins you were dating Billy Sampson and they almost died on the spot," she added.

Carrie grinned and hugged herself. "Sometimes even I feel like dying on the spot. Billy came over last night, and Graham and Claudia were playing with the kids, so I was set free. We went to the beach. . . ."

Emma nudged Carrie's arm. "And?"

"And . . . it was . . . unbelievable," Carrie admitted. "I didn't get back until three o'clock."

"Why, you little devil!" Sam laughed. "Tell us every detail."

"Well, we walked on the beach for a while, and talked about music, photography, just everything," Carrie said.

"Those aren't the kind of details Sam was looking for," Emma said with a laugh.

"Ah, she knows me so well," Sam said. "Get to the good stuff," she demanded.

"Well, we fooled around a little. . . ." Carrie hesitated.

"Fooled around with your clothes on or off?" Sam asked.

"Sam!" Emma objected. "Leave her alone! If Carrie wants to tell us, she will. It's very personal. Right, Carrie?"

"Oh, give me a break!" Sam snorted. "Did you do it or not?"

"Not, but almost," Carrie admitted.

"On the beach?" Sam screeched. "Whoa, get down, Carrie!"

"It was really, really fantastic," Carrie said, "and I definitely wanted to, but . . . I don't know. In another way I didn't want to, if that makes any sense."

Emma nodded. "It does to me. You haven't really known him that long, for one thing. I feel the same way about Kurt."

"You still haven't slept with Kurt?" Sam asked.

"No," Emma admitted. "It's a big thing for me, the first time. I want everything to be perfect."

"Sam probably can't remember that far back," Carrie teased, "can you, Sam?"

"In the immortal words of Pee-wee Herman: 'I'm rubber, you're glue, everything you say bounces off me, and sticks on you,'" Sam chanted in a singsong voice. "Besides, you're the one who's been doing it since she was sixteen."

"With one guy, whom I loved, whom I'd known forever. How old were *you*, anyway?" Carrie challenged Sam.

"Hey, look who approaches," Sam said, changing the subject quickly.

Coming toward them was Howie Lawrence, a small, thin, extremely rich guy who had a crush on Carrie. He was both nice and funny, though around Carrie he got nervous and was very insecure. Carrie only liked him as a friend.

"Now, there's the guy you should be going for," Sam counseled. "An only child, mega-rich parents—you'd be golden!"

Carrie nudged Sam in the ribs to shut her up as Howie walked up to them.

"Hi, what's happening?" Howie asked them, his eyes on Carrie.

"Not much," Carrie said, "just enjoying the sun."

"Did you guys hear about the beach party tonight?" Howie asked them.

Sam and Carrie shook their heads.

"Out at the dunes," Howie continued. "You guys should come." Again he had his eyes only on Carrie.

"Gee, I don't think so, Howie," Carrie said with a kind smile.

"The Flirts'll be there," Howie said. "Frank told me they were all planning to come." Frank was the Flirts' lead guitarist. Howie knew Carrie was dating Billy Sampson. He was willing to try and lure her to the party any way he could.

Carrie was taken aback. Billy hadn't mentioned any beach party to her. "Are you sure?" Carrie asked.

"That's what Frank said." Howie shrugged. "You know those guys are always up for a party. Listen, I have to get over to the club. So maybe I'll see you tonight."

"Billy didn't say anything about a party," Carrie said when Howie was out of earshot.

"Neither did Pres," Sam said.

"I knew about it," Emma admitted. "Kurt has to drive the taxi tonight, and then he has to study for a biology exam, otherwise we would have gone." Kurt was working two jobs and carrying eight credits during summer session, so he was often too busy to hang out.

"Should I be worried?" Carrie asked.

"Just because Howie says Billy's going doesn't mean he's going," Emma pointed out.

"Are you worried about Pres?" Carrie asked Sam.

Sam shrugged. "I don't think Pres and I are that far along yet," she admitted. "Actually, I'm not sure *what* we are."

"Well, what do you want it to be?" Emma asked.

"I don't know," Sam admitted. "Maybe it's just a physical thing, and all I want is to jump his bones."

"You mean you'd do it with a guy you didn't love?" Emma asked, wide-eyed.

"If I wanted to," Sam said. "Why should guys be the only ones who can act that way?"

"And then again, why should we stoop to their level?" Carrie asked.

"It's just not such a big deal," Sam scoffed. "For example, Pres invited me to go away with him for the weekend, and—"

"Billy invited me, too!" Carrie said excitedly. "I was just about to tell you! To the band's gig in Bangor, right?"

"Right!" Sam said. "Are you going to go?"

"Are you?" Carrie asked.

"I'm thinking about it."

"Me, too," Carrie said. "But I'll think about it a lot differently if Billy's going to beach parties without me."

"It sounds so exciting," Emma sighed. "Sometimes it seems like Kurt can never go

118

anywhere, he's so busy between school and work. And he never has any money, either."

"That's okay, Em, you have enough money to go around," Sam said brightly.

"Below the belt," Carrie murmured.

"Is this Rag-On-Emma-Because-She's-Rich Day?" Emma asked Sam.

"I'm sorry," Sam said sincerely. "It's purely envy," she admitted.

"What do we do about this beach party thing?" Carrie asked.

"How about we go and see if they show up?" Sam suggested.

"And see who they show up with," Carrie murmured.

"Do you think it will look like you're just spying on them?" Emma asked.

"No way!" Sam said. "Howie invited us. And technically we didn't even know they were going to be there—so if they are there—we make like it's a total surprise, right?"

"Right," Carrie agreed, but she still had a worried look on her face.

"Okay, here's the plan," Sam said. "We meet at the Jacobses' house at, say, ten o'clock, we make sure we look incredible, and we go over to the dunes together. Deal?"

"Deal," Emma said. "I'll be there for moral support."

"Deal," Carrie sighed. "All I can say is that life was much simpler when it was just me and Josh, and I knew for sure he loved me and I loved him."

"Yeah," Sam agreed, "but it wasn't nearly as exciting!"

EIGHT

By the time Sam got home after vegging out on the beach all day with her friends, it was early evening. For some reason, she was in a great mood. She didn't feel that concerned about Presley, and she wondered why. *Maybe I'm just not as crazy about him as Carrie is about Billy*, Sam thought.

As she ran up the stairs she could hear the twins screaming at each other at the top of their lungs.

"It is too your fault!" one of them shouted.

"Oh, yeah, like you didn't go right along with it," the other one yelled back.

Sam stood at their door, but they were too busy shrieking at each other to notice.

"Get out of my room!" Allie screamed.

"It's my room, too, you idiot!" Becky snarled back.

"Well, I don't want to share a room with you anymore," Allie ranted. "Move into the guest room!"

"*You* move into the guest room!" Becky yelled back. "Better yet, move in with Brian. He's the only person who's still speaking to you!"

"Do you two think you could hold it down to a dull roar?" Sam asked them.

"Go away," Allie said.

"My pleasure," Sam responded sweetly. "But it's my day off and I'd like to experience it without a headache from listening to you two yell."

"We can yell if we want to," Becky said. "It's our house."

"I give up," Sam said, throwing her hands in the air. "Yell! Scream! Kill each other, for all I care!" She started toward her room.

"Wait a second," Allie said quickly.

"What are you going to do, tell her?" Becky asked in disgust.

"Maybe she can help," Allie said to her sister.

"I doubt it," Becky snorted.

"Why, do you have a better idea?" Allie snapped. "You don't, so shut up!"

"Look, you two work on it and if it's still

earth-shattering tomorrow, let me know," Sam said. "Today I am officially not here. I'm going to take a bath."

Just as Sam settled down into a tub full of bubbles, the phone rang. "Ahhhhhh," she murmured happily, "it can ring off the hook for all I care, 'cause I ain't here." She sank farther down into the fragrant bubbles and closed her eyes.

"Sam!" one of the twins was yelling at the bathroom door. "It's Flash Hathaway for you!"

Flash! That was different. It had to do with her real career, not this temporary babysitting for the monsters. Sam scrambled out of the tub, threw on her robe, and ran for the phone.

"Hello?"

"Babe! You sound out of breath!" Flash said. "Doing anything I'd like to be doing?"

"If you'd like to be taking a bath," Sam said evenly. "Did you get the new contact sheets?"

"Babe, when I tell you the new shots are dynamite, I am underestimating the impact."

"Gee, great!" Sam said. Almost against her will the images flashed through her mind: the see-through material, the provocative poses, her practically naked for all the world to—

"Anyway, I didn't call you just to tell you about the contact sheets," Flash continued, interrupting Sam's thought. "I have big news for you. Really big. How would you like to do your first professional job?"

"A real booking? Are you kidding?" Sam asked.

"I kid you not," Flash said. "I been telling you, you got what it takes, babe. You got to learn to listen to the Flashman!"

"I'm listening now!" Sam assured him.

"Okay, here's the deal. It's a lingerie spread for *Uptown* magazine," Flash began.

"*Uptown* magazine!" Sam cried. "I love *Uptown!*" *Uptown* was a new glossy magazine that featured sophisticated articles, tell-all interviews with the rich and famous, and sexy fashion layouts.

"Yeah, their fashion stuff is knockout, real class," Flash agreed. "So I'm taking two models—you and another girl—to Sugarloaf for two days. We pose you against the mountains at sunrise, stuff like that, very highbrow—"

"Wait, wait a second," Sam said. "Where's Sugarloaf? Which two days?"

"Oh yeah, that's right. You're the pigeon who has barely been out of Idaho," Flash chuckled.

"I'm from Kansas, not Idaho, and I am not a pigeon," Sam said.

"You taking assertiveness training from Belinda or something?" Flash asked. "Because I got a million models who would kill for a gig like this—"

"I'm sorry," Sam said quickly. "I really do want to do it."

"That's better," Flash said. "Sugarloaf is a ski resort, about forty minutes away by plane. It's practically deserted during the summer. We leave tomorrow in the late afternoon, we come back Wednesday after the shoot. Sound good?" Flash asked.

"Sounds great!" Sam breathed. "I can hardly believe it!"

"Hey, an all-expense-paid trip to Sugarloaf, your picture in *Uptown*, and you even get paid a hundred bucks!" Flash said.

"Pinch me, I must be dreaming!" Sam exclaimed.

"I'd love to pinch you, babe," Flash laughed, "but we'll save that for Sugarloaf, if you get my meaning."

Sam didn't allow that comment to register. She was too busy thinking about the launching of her professional modeling career.

"You can get the time off, can't you?" Flash asked. "I gotta know today."

"Oh, I can. I will," Sam assured him. She

didn't know how she would, but she was absolutely not going to let this opportunity pass her by.

"Cool," Flash said. "So the limo will come by for you tomorrow at four-thirty. The plane takes off at five-thirty, we're there before six-thirty, we're in a hot tub looking out at the mountains by seven. Sound good?"

"Sounds unbelievable," Sam agreed, gripping the phone. "I can't thank you enough for choosing me for the job," she added.

"No prob, babe," Flash said breezily. "It's nice to know you're so appreciative. You can show me just exactly how appreciative tomorrow night. *Ciao!*"

Sam put the phone down in a daze and sat on her bed. This was it. This was one of those moments in life that changed everything. Maybe she really wouldn't have to go to Kansas State in the fall. Surely if her parents saw her pictures in a fashion layout in a major magazine, they'd believe she actually had a career as a model.

"Could we talk to you?" Allie asked tentatively.

The twins stood at Sam's door with serious expressions on their faces.

"I just got a professional modeling job," Sam

told them, still hardly believing it herself. "I'm going to be in *Uptown* magazine."

"For real?" Allie asked, wide-eyed.

"Uh-huh. A limo is coming to pick me up tomorrow afternoon."

"Does this mean you won't work here anymore?" Becky asked.

"Oh, I'll only be away overnight," Sam assured them. "I'll be right back here the following day."

"I guess you wish it was a longer job," Allie said.

"Sure!" Sam laughed. "Who wouldn't?"

"Come on, Becky," Allie said to her sister. "You were right."

The twins started out of the room.

"Wait a sec!" Sam called. "Right about what?"

"Never mind," Allie mumbled.

"You can talk to me, really!" Sam said. "I was only kidding before about not listening to you because it's my day off."

"No, you weren't," Becky said.

"Okay, you're right," Sam agreed reluctantly. "But I'm in a better mood now, so talk away."

Allie bit her lower lip and looked at her sister, then she seemed to make a decision.

"Well, it's about Brian and Brent, our boy-friends," she began.

"Yeah?" Sam asked.

"Well, you know how we went to the party with them the other night," Allie began. "A lot of the kids there were older and stuff. Brenda hangs out with all these high school kids. So anyway—"

The phone rang again.

"Just a sec," Sam told Allie, and answered the phone. "Hello?"

"Hi, it's Emma. I forgot what time we said we were meeting tonight."

"Ten," Sam said. "Hey, listen to my news—you're not going to believe this," she said excitedly. "Flash just called me, and I have my first professional modeling job!"

"Through Flash?" Emma asked doubtfully.

"Oh, ye of little faith," Sam intoned. "It's for *Uptown* magazine, I'll have you know. I told you Flash was okay!"

Sam went on to tell Emma everything that Flash had told her about the job. She nearly forgot about the twins in her excitement. *Just as well*, she thought when she turned around to give them the "off in five" signal and saw that they were gone.

"Oh, Sam, I'm so happy for you," Emma was

saying. "It's incredible that you got a job so quickly."

"Can you believe it?" Sam said. "Oh, and one more thing. A limo is picking me up tomorrow. A limo! The only time I was ever in a limo was that time your mother rented one when she was here!"

"You have to promise to tell me and Carrie all about it when you get back," Emma told her. "And find out what issue of *Uptown* it's going to be in so we can all buy copies."

Sam and Emma talked a little longer, then hung up. Sam decided to take a look around the house for the twins to see what it was they wanted to talk about. In the kitchen she found a scribbled note stuck to a blob of peanut butter on the counter. It read, *Gone for a walk. A & B.*

Oh well, thought Sam. *I guess if it's important, they'll tell me some other time.*

That evening Carrie and Emma met Sam right on time, and they immediately headed over to the dunes.

"Congratulations on your first professional modeling job," Carrie told Sam.

"I told her about it," Emma said hastily. "I figured you wouldn't mind."

"Of course I don't mind," Sam declared. "Thanks, Carrie."

"You must be so excited," Carrie said.

"Well, I am," Sam said. "But at the moment, I guess I'm more interested in seeing if Presley is going to show his hot body at this party."

"I don't feel good about this," Carrie said. "I think Emma was right. They're going to think we're spying on them."

"Would you relax?" Sam said. "We're going early so that even if they do show up, we'll be there first, therefore it will look like *they* are spying on *us*."

"The way your mind works is a thing of beauty," Emma told Sam admiringly.

When they reached the dunes a few kids were already there, but to their relief Billy and Pres weren't among them. Unfortunately Lorell and Daphne were.

"Well, if it isn't the Three Musketeers," Lorell trilled.

"Hi, Lorell, bye, Lorell," Sam said as they walked by, deliberately choosing a spot in the sand far away from Lorell and Daphne.

Emma shook out the old quilt the Hewitts had given her to use on the beach, and the girls all put their stuff on it. Someone had made a large bonfire, and even from far away the girls could see Daphne and Lorell arguing by the light of the flames.

"I wonder what they're arguing about," Carrie mused.

"Maybe they knocked off Diana and they're trying to decide which one of them takes the fall," Sam said.

Emma laughed. "Oh, I think both of them should get sent away for life. Then all three of them would be gone, and my life would be greatly improved."

"Don't look now," Carrie said to Sam, "but Daphne is pointing at you. Uh-oh, now she's heading this way."

"Great," Sam groaned. "Just what I need."

"Listen, I have something to say to you," Daphne said belligerently, standing over Sam.

Daphne didn't look at all well. In fact, she looked noticeably worse than usual. It hardly seemed possible, but she appeared even more emaciated than she normally did. Her hair looked dry and brittle, and her arms hung like sticks out of her sleeveless shirt. Her face was gaunt, and the dark-circled eyes sunken in her face glittered with a wild look.

"So say it," Sam said.

"It's your fault that I'm not modeling the wedding dress in the finale of the fashion show."

"What are you talking about?" Sam asked her.

"Yeah, like you don't know," Daphne snorted. "Kimmy broke her ankle, and she can't be in the show. I worked my butt off so I could take her place and fit into the wedding gown for the show. But Pam turned me down. She said the only girl on the island who could fit into Kimmy's dress without alterations is you. I know what she means. She means I'm too fat. But if it weren't for you, she would have used a different wedding gown and I would have modeled it!"

Carrie and Emma just stared at Daphne with their jaws practically in the sand. They had no idea what she was babbling about. On the other hand, they had caught that "I'm too fat" remark. Something was very, very wrong with this girl.

"Listen, Daphne, I had nothing to do with it," Sam said. "I'm not even in that fashion show, and you are, so I don't know what you're bitching about."

Daphne narrowed her eyes and ran her shaking hand through her hair. "I know what you're thinking. You're thinking, how can a pig like me be in a fashion show?"

Sam stood up and looked at Daphne closely.

"Daphne, no one's thinking that. No one's thinking anything. Are you okay?"

"Of course I'm okay," Daphne said hotly. "Or I *would* be if you'd stop talking about me!"

"I really think you need some help, Daphne," Sam said quietly. "Are you . . . are you on anything?"

"I brought you your jacket," Lorell said, coming up next to Daphne.

Daphne ignored her. "Did someone tell you I was on something?" she asked Sam.

"No, but you don't look well," Sam said. "I thought maybe—"

"You think I look fat. Isn't that what you think?" Daphne practically spat at Sam.

"Hey, listen, you really need some help, Daphne," Sam said, taking a step backward. She looked at Lorell. "You're supposed to be her friend. Why don't you do something to help her?"

"It's really none of your business," Lorell said coolly. "Maybe where you come from people talk about their private concerns to every piece of trash who floats by, but that's not how we do things."

Sam just shook her head in disbelief. "Lorell, when you look at yourself in the mirror, do you like what you see?"

Lorell didn't answer. She just led Daphne back to their blanket.

"That poor girl," Emma said. "She's really sick."

"Yeah, and Daphne's pretty messed up, too," Sam joked.

"Ha ha," Emma said. "I mean it. Something is seriously wrong with Daphne. Aside from her obvious anorexia."

"And what was all that stuff about modeling a wedding gown?" Carrie asked.

Sam quickly explained what Pam Winslow had told her about the wedding fashions scheduled to close the fashion show that Saturday. "So I'm the only girl Pam knows who's tall and thin enough to fit into the thing," she concluded.

"You should do it!" Carrie said. "Why won't you?"

"Hi, Carrie!" Howie Lawrence called out, running over to the girls' blanket. "Hey, I didn't expect to see you here!"

"Well, I changed my mind," Carrie said.

"You girls want a beer or a Coke or anything?" Howie asked. "I've got a coolerful."

They all asked for Cokes, and Howie scampered away to get them.

"Wow, who is that?" Emma asked, squinting at a faraway blanket where two intertwined bodies were rolling around passionately on a blanket.

Just at that moment, the female body shook her head and laughed at something.

"It's Kristy," Carrie said. "I'd recognize that bleached blond hair anywhere." Kristy was a long-legged, sexy girl of about twenty who lived on the island year-round. She wrote a column for *Breakers*, the island newspaper, that delivered the inside scoop on everything that happened on the island. She was also known for being wild.

"I don't think she has her shirt on!" Emma whispered, squinting into the distance.

Howie had started back to the girls with their Cokes but stopped in front of Kristy's blanket. "Hey, man, how's it going?" Howie asked in a loud voice. "When are the Flirts gonna be at the Play Café again?"

Carrie clutched at Sam's arm and gasped. "Oh my God, it's Billy. I know it's Billy!"

"We won't be back at the Play Café for a couple of weeks. We've got some gigs out of town," a male voice said.

But Carrie was wrong. It wasn't Billy. And Sam didn't need to see who sat up next to Kristy to know who it was. Because the voice that had answered Howie had a soft, unmistakeable Tennessee twang.

NINE

"I'm leaving," Sam said, reaching for her bag.

"It probably doesn't mean anything," Carrie said. "I mean, we can't really see over there that well. Maybe it's not what it looks like."

"Cokes for one and all," Howie said, arriving and plopping down on the girls' blanket.

"I gotta go," Sam said.

"I'll go with you," Emma offered.

"No!" Carrie said quickly. She did not want to be left alone on a blanket with Howie, whether Billy turned up or not. "If you're leaving, we're all leaving."

"But you just got here!" Howie protested.

"Yeah, well, I'm feeling a little sick to my stomach," Sam said, getting up. Carrie and Emma got up with her. Howie just sat there with a forlorn look on his face.

"Sorry, Howie, but I have to take the quilt," Emma said.

"Oh, sure," Howie said, scrambling up. "Are you positive you can't stay?" Howie asked Carrie. "Most of the really cool people aren't even here yet."

"The really cool people?" Sam repeated as she helped Emma fold the quilt. "That is one of the stupidest remarks I've ever heard."

"Sam!" Carrie objected.

"I'm sorry, Howie," Sam sighed. "I'm just . . . I have to get out of here." She stomped through the sand toward the car, and Emma and Carrie followed her.

"I'm really sorry," Carrie said quietly when the three of them were sitting in the car.

"Why?" Sam asked. "You didn't do anything. Besides, now I know the truth. And to think I almost went away with him for the weekend!"

"Maybe we're jumping to conclusions," Emma said. "Remember when I saw Kurt out with another girl, and I went crazy, and it turned out to be his sister?"

Sam just stared at Emma. "Kristy is not Presley's sister. And even if she were, that wouldn't stop her."

"Maybe you like Pres more than you thought," Carrie said. "Otherwise you wouldn't be so upset."

"I don't know what I thought," Sam sighed. "I thought . . . I thought he wouldn't want to be with Kristy, that's for sure." She started the car and drove toward town. "I thought he'd be a little discerning, at least. Show a little taste. I thought . . . I thought he'd be so crazy about me that he wouldn't even think about anyone else," she admitted.

"Even though you're not sure you're that crazy about him?" Carrie asked.

"So sue me, I've got an ego," Sam said.

"Want to go over to the Play Café?" Emma asked.

"I think I just want to go home," Sam said. "I still haven't figured out how to get permission from Mr. Jacobs to be away overnight tomorrow night. I guess I'll go work on that one."

When Sam walked in the door she happened to glance into the den and saw Mr. Jacobs and his girlfriend passionately kissing on the couch. Sam tried to tiptoe by, but Mr. Jacobs heard her.

"Hi, Sam! Come in and meet Stephanie," Mr. Jacobs called to her.

"Oh, I don't want to interrupt," Sam said.

"Nonsense! Come on in! Stephanie, this is our wonderful au pair I told you about, Samantha Bridges. Sam, this is Stephanie Kramer."

Stephanie looked to be in her early thirties. She was very pretty in a natural-looking way, with wavy brown hair, brown eyes, and a great smile.

"Hi, Sam, call me Stephanie," she said with a friendly smile. That was funny, since Sam still called Dan Jacobs Mr. Jacobs. "I've heard great things about you."

"Oh well, in that case it's all true," Sam said breezily.

Mr. Jacobs laughed harder than Sam's joke warranted. Sam looked at him closely. He was really a very nice-looking man. Tonight he looked flushed, happy, and years younger than he looked when he was worrying about the twins.

"So, how's everything going with the girls?" Mr. Jacobs asked.

"Oh, fine," Sam said.

"Tell Steph how great they can be," Mr. Jacobs coaxed. "She's only met them once."

"Well, they're . . . great, all right," Sam said.

"I can't even tell you what a huge difference Sam has made in their lives," Mr. Jacobs told Stephanie. "They're really turning into young ladies. Right, Sam?"

"Right," Sam echoed. *Well, it's now or never,*

Sam thought. *Mr. Jacobs was in a great mood.* In fact, for him he was probably delirious with joy. Mr. Jacobs was not exactly known for his forthcoming personality.

"Uh, Mr. Jacobs, I was wondering . . . I have an opportunity to do a modeling shoot for *Uptown* magazine, and—"

"Really?" Stephanie interjected, obviously impressed. "I love that magazine!"

"Me, too," Sam agreed. "Anyway, it's a big opportunity for me, but it would mean being away from late afternoon tomorrow until the following evening."

"I don't think that would be a problem," Mr. Jacobs said slowly. "Say, I've got an idea! Why don't you stay over tomorrow night, Steph? That way we can spend some real quality time with the girls, just like a family."

The look on the older woman's face told Sam just what Stephanie thought of that idea. "Maybe it's a little soon for that," she began.

"No, I think it would be great!" Mr. Jacobs said. He hugged Stephanie's shoulder. "I know you're a little nervous about it, but you'll see. Being here overnight will make it easier. Everyone will start acting more naturally around one another!"

Poor Stephanie, Sam thought as she climbed

upstairs to her room. *Poor me, too,* she thought, thinking about Pres with Kristy. As she walked by the twins' bedroom, she thought she heard the sound of crying, and she stopped and listened.

Someone *was* crying. Sam knocked softly on the door.

"It's me," Sam whispered. "Can I come in?"

"Go away," said a tear-filled voice.

Sam stood with her hand on the doorknob, unsure about what to do.

"Are you crying?" Sam whispered again.

"None of your business," the voice responded.

Sam sighed. "Are you sure you don't want to talk about it?"

"Well . . ." another voice said.

"No!" the first voice said firmly. "Go away."

Sam hesitated again. She truly did not know if she should go in anyway, but finally she decided against it. After all, they did have a right to their privacy, she figured.

Sam threw herself on her bed, utterly exhausted. Between dealing with guys and dealing with the twins, life was very complicated. The only thing that was going exactly the way she wanted it to was her modeling career.

Visions of Sugarloaf danced through Sam's

head. She'd be posing in some gorgeous night-gown, her hair and makeup perfect. In the background, the sun would just be rising over the mountains, the light glinting through her red curls. The shots would appear in *Uptown*, and Flash's phone would start ringing off the hook. "Who is that girl? We've got to get that girl!" Soon her face would be on the cover of *Cosmopolitan*, her name a household word. She'd travel to every corner of the globe and make so much money she'd be richer than Emma. Presley would call her and beg to see her again, but she'd just laugh and tell him that between the European prince who was crazy about her and the major rock star who wanted to marry her, she really had so little free time. . . .

"Sam, we're hungry!" Someone was yelling outside her door and knocking insistently.

"It's the middle of the—" Sam started to say, but then she opened her eyes and realized it was morning. She'd fallen asleep with her clothes on, and had never even gotten under the covers.

"Sam!" one of the twins called again, pounding harder on the door.

"Jeez, give it a rest!" Sam yelled irritably. "Go get some cereal or something, okay? I'll be down in five minutes."

Sam quickly washed her face, brushed her teeth, and changed her clothes. She'd have to shower later. When she ran downstairs, the twins were sitting at the breakfast table with their father, drinking orange juice and eating cornflakes.

"Sorry I overslept," Sam told Mr. Jacobs.

"No problem," Mr. Jacobs said. "The girls are really old enough to get their own breakfast, aren't you, girls?"

Neither twin deigned to answer their father. They just continued eating.

"So, I told the twins about Stephanie coming over tonight to spend the night, and they're real excited."

"Yeah, real," Becky said in a flat voice.

"Is she staying in your room?" Allie challenged her father.

"No, of course not," he said, obviously flustered. "She'll stay in the guest room."

"Look, if the two of you are already doing it, she doesn't need to stay in the guest room on our account," Becky spat out. "It's not like we're children."

Sam poured water in the coffeemaker and kept her mouth shut. The monsters seemed even worse than usual lately. Something was definitely going on with them.

"In this house people who aren't married do not stay in the same room," Mr. Jacobs said evenly. "And as far as your *other* remark, that is not something I care to hear my young ladies discuss."

"Dad, that's practically prehistoric," Allie told her father.

"Well, that's my feeling and I am your father," Mr. Jacobs said. He picked up the morning paper and took it with him to the den.

"I hate him," Allie said flatly, "and I hate his stupid girlfriend even more."

Sam poured a cup of coffee and sat down. "Listen, your dad is a nice guy, and he really loves you," Sam said.

The twins didn't say a word.

"Is there something bothering you two that you want to talk about?" Sam asked. "I know you guys were really upset about something last night."

Allie and Becky just glared at Sam, and then marched up to their room.

Well, you can't get blood from a stone, Sam thought. *I guess they'll talk when they're ready.*

It was four o'clock, and Sam was just finishing packing when the phone rang.

"Hey, how's it goin'?" Pres asked her in his lazy drawl.

"Fine," Sam answered tersely.

"Did I catch you at a bad time?" he asked, hearing the frost in her voice.

"Yes, actually. I'm just about to leave for a modeling job out of town. The limo is picking me up in half-hour."

"You didn't mention that you modeled," Pres said. "But I sure do think you're a perfect candidate."

"Thanks," Sam said.

"Well, I won't keep you. I just wondered if you'd given some thought to this weekend," Pres said.

"I think you should invite Kristy," Sam said.

Silence. "Pardon me?"

"You looked awfully friendly with her last night at the beach party. So why don't you invite her, seeing as the two of you are so close and all?"

"You were at the beach party?" Pres said.

"Uh-huh."

"Kristy's not important, Sam," Pres told her. "I mean, the girl is wild. She's just out for a good time."

"Yeah? So what does that say about your taste?" Sam challenged him.

146

"Look, I'm sorry you saw that last night," Pres said. "But you and I are just startin' to get to know each other. It's a little premature for you to have a say about what I do with my time."

"Then it's a little premature for you to be inviting me away for the weekend," Sam shot back.

"Maybe so," Pres conceded. "But I thought you were more sophisticated than that. You come on like you are, you know."

"What's that supposed to mean?" Sam asked. "You thought I was another Kristy?"

"No, that's not what I meant at all," Pres said.

"Look, I gotta go," Sam told him briskly.

"When will you be back?"

"Tomorrow night." Sam said good-bye and hung up. *Men*, she thought with disgust. She was sure Pres only wanted her because she wasn't sure she wanted him. If she were crazy for him, he'd be running in the other direction.

The doorbell rang, and Sam ran to the window. A sleek black stretch limo was in the driveway.

"I can't believe it!" Sam screeched with pleasure. She wished someone she knew was around to see her get into the limo. Unfortunately the twins were at a friend's house and Mr. Jacobs had gone to pick up Stephanie.

Sam grabbed her overnight case, ran down the stairs, and opened the front door. A uniformed chauffeur stood there with his hat in his hand.

"Ms. Bridges?"

"Yes."

"Let me get that for you." The chauffeur took Sam's small suitcase and put it in the trunk. Then he held the car door open for her.

"Yo, babe!" Flash said when Sam climbed into the back of the limo. He put his arm around her shoulder and squeezed. "You up for this?"

"Totally," Sam agreed.

Sitting on the other side of Flash was a gorgeous brunette in a skintight red catsuit with strategic mesh inserts and red high heels. Sitting opposite were Belinda and Leonard.

"You know Beli and Len," Flash said, gesturing toward them with his ring-bedecked fingers. Belinda looked as unhappy as usual; Leonard was his normal, obliviously cheerful self. "And this knockout is Bambi," Flash continued. "She's the other model on the shoot."

"Hi," Sam said, smiling at Bambi.

"Hi!" Bambi said with a megawatt grin. She

looked as if she were just as excited and inexperienced as Sam was, which made Sam feel more comfortable.

Flash opened a bottle of champagne and handed glasses all around. He poured some into everyone's glass.

"Here's to a wild time!" Flash said, sipping his champagne. "And I do mean wild!"

The limo quickly brought them to a private airfield, where a small four-or-six-seater airplane was waiting to fly them to Sugarloaf.

"A private plane?" Bambi giggled, tottering around on her extremely high heels.

"Hey, American Airlines doesn't stop on Sunset Island," Flash laughed. "What'd ya think we'd take?"

"Gee, I don't know," Bambi said. "Who's driving?"

"You mean flying," Belinda corrected her, a pained look on her face. "Or did you think we were going to taxi all the way to Sugarloaf?"

"Oh, I guess not," Bambi said with another giggle.

Oh, great, Sam thought. *Bambi is an airhead. I was hoping to make a friend.*

Leonard and Flash climbed into the small plane, then Flash held out his hand to assist the women up the steps. Bambi came first, unsteady on her shoes, and Flash grabbed her butt as she stepped into the cabin.

"That'll help steady you, babe," Flash said.

Bambi squealed in mock outrage.

Next he helped Sam up the steps. He reached for Sam's butt, too, but she managed to feint slightly to the left so that his hand barely grazed her. Flash seemed to think this was a game, and he wagged a finger at her. "Naughty, naughty!" he said with a grin on his face.

Next he helped Belinda up the steps. His other hand reached out for her butt. "Don't even think about it," Belinda spat out, pulling her hand from his.

"What can I say? Beli is an ice cube!" Flash said, winking at Sam. Leonard laughed, Bambi squealed, and Sam was thinking that actually Belinda was the only one there she even remotely liked.

Stop that, Sam, she told herself. *Are you nuts? This is the opportunity of a lifetime, so quit being so judgmental*. When Flash buckled up next to her, she gave him her most winning smile.

"You ever been on a private plane before?" Flash asked Sam.

"No. I love it!" Sam said, and she really did.

She could see the captain and all the instruments on the panel in the cockpit. She could even see out of the front window, the same view that the captain could see. "Maybe I'll get a pilot license one day," Sam mused.

Flash draped his arm around her and let his hand dangle dangerously close to her left breast. "Hey, babe, with a face and a body like yours, all you need to do is wet your lips and look good."

"That's obnoxious," Sam said before she could stop herself.

"What did I say?" Flash asked, sounding totally bewildered.

"I have a brain, you know," Sam said.

Flash grinned knowingly and opened another bottle of champagne. "Lemme ask you a question. You think you're here right now on account of your brain?"

"No, I suppose not," Sam conceded.

"You suppose correctly," Flash said. "You models kill me! You're like 'Look at me! Look at me!' And then when we do, you get all huffy about it." He handed her a new champagne glass. "Have some love bubbles, it'll mellow you out," Flash said, pouring her some more champagne.

"This is unbelievable!" Bambi cried from the

seat in front of them. She sat facing Sam and Flash, with Leonard next to her and Belinda alone in a seat on the other side of the very narrow aisle. "I can see everything down there! Little cars, little houses—it looks like a Monopoly game!"

"I love your enthusiasm," Leonard told her, throwing an arm around her shoulder.

"Oh, Lenny," she purred, nuzzling his neck.

"Hey, I'm only giving you six hours to stop that!" Leonard told her. Bambi laughed and started nibbling on Leonard's ear.

At first Sam just ignored them and sipped her champagne while she stared out the window. When Lenny got a blanket and threw it over them, and it became apparent that Bambi was wiggling out of her catsuit, Sam tried to catch Belinda's eye. But Belinda had her head buried in a magazine.

"Uh, gee, Bambi and Leonard seem to know each other really well," Sam said tentatively.

"You could say they're about to become bosom buddies!" Flash guffawed.

"Have they been . . . uh, going out a long time?" Sam asked.

"What's 'going out' mean?" Flash asked. "They met, like, last week or something."

Leonard and Bambi had completely disap-

152

peared under the blanket. The heavy breathing seemed to be inspiring Flash, who leaned over to Sam and started to nibble on her ear.

"I hate that," Sam said, pulling away from him.

"I like 'em feisty," Flash said with a grin. "You just tell me what turns you on, babe. I live to serve."

Bambi made a breathy moaning noise under the blanket, which was actually starting to move up and down. Sam's face burned with embarrassment.

"I guess old Leonard's initiating her into the Mile High Club."

"Which is?" Sam asked.

"People who make it in airplanes," Flash said. "Me, I prefer to big, bouncy bed. How about you, babe?"

"I prefer privacy, that's for sure," Sam said, trying to look anywhere except at the heaving blanket opposite her.

"I knew you were a class act," Flash said, running his hand over her thigh. He moved closer to Sam. "Hey, Leonard and Bambi were made for each other," he confided. "This way the trip is fun for everyone, if you get my drift."

"That's why you hired Bambi?" Sam asked. "For Leonard?"

"She's also great-looking, with a great bod," Flash said. "But yeah, I picked her for him. This way everyone has fun, and everyone is happy." He looked over at Belinda. "Except Beli. Beli's never happy," he added.

"Stop calling me that," Belinda said, not raising her eyes from her magazine.

Flash just laughed and put his arm back around Sam. "Ignore her. She's permanently on the rag, but she's a great makeup artist." He leaned close to Sam again. "Did I tell you how great-looking your boobs were in those shots?" he growled.

"No," Sam said.

"Well, they were. And believe me, the Flashman has seen many a pair of hooters in his life. I mean, they aren't big, but they are perky, kinda insolent." Flash's hand was now actually grazing Sam's breast. He leaned even closer and whispered in her ear, "I can't wait to get my hands on those puppies, and on all the rest of you, too, babe. I kid you not."

Sam pulled as far away from him as space and her seat belt would allow. The sounds from under the blanket were growing louder. "Look, Flash, I'm here as a model," she said. "The rest isn't in the job description."

He laughed. "Feisty! I told you, I like that.

Just promise me you'll be this feisty once we hit the horizontal."

"No offense, Flash, but I'm not interested in you like that," Sam said.

Flash looked at Sam as if she had just grown horns.

"Hey, babe, enough is enough," Flash said.

"What are you talking about?" Sam asked him.

"As you so recently pointed out to me, babe, stupid you ain't," Flash said. "Now you're gonna pretend like you don't know what's going on?"

Sam gulped hard. She felt dizzy from the champagne. "Look, you said you were hiring me for a professional modeling job," she began slowly.

"And I am," Flash said. "But you want to play the tune, you got to pay the piper. In other words, no nookie, no bookie."

"In other words, you just assumed I'd sleep with you," Sam said.

"Yeah, like you didn't know the deal," Flash snorted. "Like I didn't do everything except draw you a freakin' diagram."

"I didn't agree to that," Sam said hotly. She undid her seat belt, as if she could jump from the plane.

"Please, save the prissy little indignant act, okay?" Flash sneered. "My hands have been all over you like braille. You posed for me practically naked and you loved it. No one forced you."

"But you said—"

"I said what?" Flash challenged her. "You made your own choices, little girl. Lie to yourself if you want to, babe, but don't bother handing that b.s. to me."

Sam gulped and tried not to let Flash see that her hands were shaking. "I want to go home," she said evenly.

"Oh, great," Flash groaned. "Just freakin' great."

"I mean it," Sam said.

"Would you chill?" Flash said.

"No, I won't 'chill,'" Sam said. "This . . . this is not professional behavior. I'll report you to . . . someone. To Universal Models, that's who!"

"Listen, you little slut," Flash hissed between clenched teeth, "you will not report me to anyone, do you hear me? Because if you do, I will make your life hell. This is standard operating procedure for the modeling business. You're just too stupid to know it."

"No, it isn't," said a voice from across the aisle. Belinda stared at Flash.

"Don't get into this, Beli, I'm warning you," Flash said.

"It's not standard," Belinda said, "and you should be reported. In fact, I should have done it a long time ago."

The plane dipped as the pilot approached the airfield at Sugarloaf.

"No one would believe you," Flash said. "Everyone knows I dropped you—"

"Maybe they wouldn't have believed me, but they'll believe me and Sam together," Belinda said.

"What is the big deal?" Flash fumed. "I didn't rape anybody! I didn't force anybody!"

"No, you just use coercion and manipulation," Belinda said. "You just take great pictures and make every girl think she's got a chance at being a superstar, and so they go along with you."

The plane landed smoothly and taxied down the runway.

"I want this pilot to fly me back," Sam said.

"Me, too," Belinda added.

"You I couldn't care less about," Flash said to Sam, "but Beli, I need you for the shoot. There's big bucks riding on this, Beli!"

Belinda unbuckled her seat belt and stood up. "My name, you ungrateful toad, is Belinda!"

"Jeez, you babes get so hot about everything!" Flash began.

Sam grabbed the half-full bottle of champagne. "No, you're the one who's getting hot, *babe*, so I hope this cools you off." She poured the champagne into his lap.

At the sound of Flash's yelp, Bambi finally stuck her head out from under the blanket. She saw Belinda and Sam standing around Flash while he danced around, wiping viciously at his soaking-wet crotch.

"Wow," Bambi giggled, "that was some ride!"

TEN

"You are off this job, both of you!" Flash yelled at Sam and Belinda.

Leonard stuck his head out from under the blanket. "What's happening, boss?" Flash asked.

"I'm shipping these two bimbos home," Flash said.

"But, boss, what'll we do without—" Leonard began.

"We'll find somebody to be the stylist and to do the makeup—Jelly-Belly ain't exactly irreplaceable," Flash snarled. "And as for Miss Tease of the Year, she doesn't really have what it takes up front to do lingerie. We'll use Bambi for all the shots," Flash decided.

"Oh, gee!" said Bambi, wide-eyed.

"And we'll double your pay, Bambi. That

ought to make you happy enough to spread your sunshine all over, if you catch my drift."

"Sure," said Bambi, but she sounded anything but sure. She sounded a little scared.

"Listen," Belinda said to Bambi, "you can come back with us. You don't have to do anything you don't want to do."

"But I'm going to be in *Uptown* magazine!" Bambi protested.

"There'll be other opportunities," Sam told her. "If you've really got what it takes to be a model, you don't have to put up with any strings being attached." Sam knew she was talking to herself at least as much as she was talking to Bambi.

Everyone stood there looking at Bambi, waiting to see what she would do.

"I . . . I want to stay," Bambi whispered. "Thanks, anyway."

Leonard beamed and threw his arm around Bambi's shoulder. Since she was a good six inches taller than him in her high heels, this was not easy to accomplish.

"Now, there's a babe who knows what's happening," Flash said, grinning his approval. Flash looked up at the cockpit, where the pilot was waiting for instructions. "Take the broads back to the island," Flash told the pilot. "You got fuel?"

"Yes, sir," the pilot said.

Flash climbed out of the plane. Leonard and Bambi climbed out after him. "You're gonna be sorry you crossed me, both of you!" he yelled into the plane at Sam and Belinda.

The pilot got on the radio to get permission from the tower for takeoff. Sam watched Bambi, Leonard, and Flash walk toward the waiting limo, and it was like watching all her dreams go up in smoke. Then Sam saw the look on Belinda's face. As bad as she felt, she knew Belinda felt worse.

"That's the second time you've saved my skin," Sam said to her.

"I told you, I didn't do it—"

"For me," Sam finished for her. "I know. But I want to thank you, anyway."

The pilot got permission for takeoff, and the engines revved.

The two girls didn't speak again until the plane was airborne.

"You know the worst part?" Belinda whispered, staring out the window.

"What?" Sam asked.

"I compromised everything I believe in," Belinda said. "At first I did it just so I could be a model. And then I did it so I could be with Flash. I thought I loved that sleazy creep—which just shows you who the real jerk is."

"I don't exactly feel brilliant myself," Sam sighed. "I feel like a total fool."

"Well, you're not," Belinda said. "You're the one who walked away."

"I thought I was going to have this big career as a model," Sam said. "I thought my life was going to change."

"Maybe it is," Belinda said. "Maybe mine is, too. But speaking for myself, I plan to change it on my terms—or at least I'm going to try."

The girls called the car service to come pick them up when they returned to Sunset Island. Sam just hoped that it wouldn't be Kurt who picked them up. She wasn't ready to explain anything.

"I feel like such an idiot going back to the Jacobses' house," Sam said. "They don't expect me back until tomorrow night. They've got all this family stuff planned."

"Want to come to my apartment?" Belinda asked.

"Oh no," Sam said. "I wasn't hinting—"

"You'd be doing me a favor," Belinda said quickly, not looking Sam in the eye. "I really don't want to be alone."

"Okay, then," Sam said softly. She tried to laugh. "After all, I've got off until tomorrow night. I might as well take advantage of it."

Sam got her wish—a guy she didn't know showed up to drive them to Belinda's apartment. It turned out to be a slightly rundown fifth-floor walkup studio apartment.

"I know it's not much, but renting a place on Sunset Island costs a mint," Belinda said, putting down her suitcase.

"Hey, at least it's yours," Sam pointed out. "This is the first time in my life I've lived anywhere except my parents' house in Junction, Kansas." Sam flopped down on the well-worn sofa. "So, what are you going to do now?" Sam asked her. "Do you know?"

"Well, first we're going to report Flash to Universal Models and the Better Business Bureau. You were serious about that, weren't you?" Belinda asked.

"Absolutely," Sam agreed.

"After that . . . I don't have a clue," Belinda confessed. "One thing is for sure, I can't stay on Sunset Island without big bucks."

"Maybe you could get a job at the Play Café or something," Sam suggested. "Speaking of which, I'm starving. Want to order a pizza? My treat."

The girls ordered a large pizza, and stayed up most of the night eating and talking. By the time Sam fell asleep on the threadbare sofa, she didn't feel quite as terrible about everything, or quite as alone.

Sam spent the next day walking around the old part of the island, where she was sure she wouldn't run into anybody she knew. Frankly, she was depressed. She'd just turned her back on what was maybe the opportunity of a lifetime. After all, no one else was offering her a chance to model in *Uptown* magazine. Maybe Flash's way really *was* how things were done. Maybe she had just made the stupidest mistake of her life.

In the late afternoon Sam hopped the trolley back to the Jacobses' house. When she got there only the twins were home. They were making microwave brownies in the kitchen.

"Sam!" Allie exclaimed when she walked in.

"Sam!" Becky echoed. They stared at her wide-eyed.

"Gee, I was only away overnight," Sam said. "Nice to know you missed me."

"I want you to know that we don't think you should get fired. We're completely on your side."

"Huh?" Sam said. "What are you talking about?"

"Dad is ready to fire you," Allie said, "for what you did."

164

Sam sat down, her heart thudding in her chest. "What did I do wrong?"

Becky finished mixing the brownies, and she shoved the pan into the microwave. "You know, what you did with that photographer guy," she said.

"Am I losing my mind?" Sam asked. "I didn't do anything with him!"

"Well, that's not what Dad thinks," Allie said.

"Look, start from the beginning," Sam demanded. "You're driving me nuts."

Allie sat down across from Sam. "We went out to lunch with Dad and his girlfriend a few hours ago," Allie explained. "We went over to Victor's—you know, that big old place near the Sunset Inn."

"And?" Sam said impatiently.

"Well, you know how at night they have all kinds of wild parties in the private club upstairs over the restaurant—"

"I didn't know that," Sam said. "I've never been there!"

"Well, we know about it," Becky said coolly. "Anyway, we'd heard about it. So while Dad and Stephanie were having coffee, we pretended we were going to the ladies' room, and we snuck upstairs. We just wanted to see it," she explained.

"Right!" Allie said. "And when we got upstairs we saw this big sign. Flashman's Hot-Flush Babes, it said. And there were these real sexy pictures all over the walls, and a lot of them were of you."

Sam felt like she was going to throw up. "Of me?" she asked faintly.

"Uh-huh," Becky said. "Of course, some other girl seemed like she was the star, but a sign said she dances there for private parties, so I guess that's why. Anyway, *she* didn't have any clothes on at all!"

"Becky's the one who blew your cover," Allie said.

"I did not!" Becky yelled. "You told him about it first, so then I just showed him."

"Anyway, we both think it's totally cool," Allie said.

"Yeah, totally cool," Becky echoed.

The bell went off on the microwave and Becky retrieved the brownies. "Want a brownie?" she asked Sam.

"No," said Sam. The sweet smell of the brownies was making her feel even sicker. This just couldn't be happening to her!

"Anyway," Becky said, cutting into the hot brownies, "we just want you to know we think it was awesome, even if Dad is ready to kill you."

"He's really going to fire me?" Sam said in a tiny voice.

"We told him we don't want him to," Allie said.

The front door opened and Sam heard footsteps in the front hall.

"Hello," Mr. Jacobs said hollowly when he saw Sam. "I think we need to have a talk."

With a sinking heart, Sam followed Mr. Jacobs into the den. She was surprised to find that Stephanie was already there. Stephanie gave her a small, understanding smile.

"Did the twins tell you what happened at lunch today?" Mr. Jacobs asked.

"Yes," Sam said.

"I guess I don't need to tell you how shocked I am," he said. "I suppose you never thought I'd see that smut, and it was only by chance that I did—"

"Listen, Mr. Jacobs, I haven't even seen those photos myself," Sam began.

"I don't know what makes you think that matters," Mr. Jacobs said. "You obviously posed for them, so you know what kind of photos I'm talking about. Frankly, I'm shocked at your lack of modesty."

"But I didn't even know about this!" Sam protested. "I do too have modesty."

"What are you trying to say?" Mr. Jacobs asked.

"I had no idea there were pictures of me on display! I never gave anyone permission to do that!" she cried passionately.

"Let me get this straight," said Mr. Jacobs. "You posed for those sleazy shots of your own free will, correct?"

"I didn't think they would be sleazy, honest, Mr. Jacobs. They were for . . . for my modeling portfolio." Sam felt like crying with rage and humiliation. It was so unfair!

"Sam, you were photographed wearing extremely revealing undergarments, is that correct? You posed in those outfits?"

"Yes, I did," Sam whispered.

"And you probably signed a release form of some kind, right?"

"Right," Sam admitted miserably. "But I didn't know he could do whatever he wanted with them! I never thought they'd be—"

"It doesn't seem to me you did very much thinking at all," Mr. Jacobs said. He rubbed his forehead wearily. "And you know the worst part?" he went on. "The twins admire you for it. Admire you! They want to emulate you in everything. What kind of an example are you setting?"

"Look, Mr. Jacobs, this isn't what it looks like," Sam said in desperation. "I never really did anything bad! I mean, I posed for the pictures, that's true, but that's all! I guess I used bad judgment, but . . ."

"You guess?" He stared at her incredulously.

"I just didn't understand he could use the photos in such a sleazy way, without my even knowing about it. I thought they were for my portfolio. . . ." Sam faltered. "It . . . it makes me look like something I'm not."

"Well, that's the other part of it, Sam. It's not only the fact that these pictures are on display in a disreputable nightclub. This so-called modeling career of yours . . . I mean, if that's the kind of modeling you want to do, then I'm afraid I misjudged the kind of girl you are. I think I have to let you go, Sam," Mr. Jacobs said. He sighed heavily. "I'm sorry, but my girls are too important to me."

Sam gulped hard to hold back her tears. "I'll go pack," she said, getting up from the sofa. She was not going to beg for her job. She was not going to sit there and defend herself. Mr. Jacobs was going to think whatever he wanted, anyway.

"Wait!" said Stephanie. She put her hand on Mr. Jacobs's arm. "I think you should reconsider."

"Stephanie!" Mr. Jacobs objected.

"Well, that's what I think," she said. "Look, you wanted me to be more involved in the twins' lives, and this certainly affects their lives. I think we should talk about this some more."

"All right," Mr. Jacobs agreed in a steely voice. "You and I will discuss it privately. Sam, would you mind waiting in your room?"

Sam left the study and walked wearily upstairs. Just yesterday everything in her life had looked so terrific. Now everything was a nightmare.

"Yeah, so?" One of the twins was yelling when Sam walked by their room. The door was open, and Sam could see that Becky was yelling into the phone. "He's a total liar. I never went to third base with him! I never even went to second base with him!"

Sam stopped in her tracks. Roughly translated, she knew, *second base* meant anything above the waist, and *third base* meant everything below it.

"Well, he's a liar, too!" Becky screamed. "My sister didn't do anything! We just gave them our bras, and that's all!"

Just gave them their bras? Sam mouthed. What were the twins up to?

"Well, I don't care what everyone's saying," Becky yelled. "You can just go to hell, Brenda!" She slammed the phone down hard.

Allie put the pillow over her head. "I hate her," she cried. "I want to die."

Sam walked into their room. "Won't you please talk to me about what's going on?" she asked them.

"We *tried* to talk to you," Becky said angrily, "but you were too *busy*."

"*I'll* tell you," Allie said, lifting the pillow from her tear-stained face. "I don't care if Becky wants me to or not. When we went to that party with Brian and Brent, there were a lot of older kids there that Brenda hangs out with. Some of the kids were drinking, and trying to act cool."

"Yeah, like Brent and Brian, for example," Becky said.

"So this girl told Brian and Brent that we weren't fifteen like we said, that we were really only thirteen, and everyone laughed. They said we were too young for them, and we said we weren't, and they told us to prove it," Allie continued. "They said we should give them our bras, so we did. At the time it seemed totally cool. I mean, they paid a lot of attention to us and everything, and they're sixteen!"

"But now they won't give them back," Becky said. "They've been showing them to everyone, saying that we went almost all the way with them. They said they have our panties, too, which they don't. And everyone knows they're our bras because they're totally identical, and they still have our names inside from camp last summer."

"That's awful!" Sam exclaimed.

"Yeah, and no one believes us," Allie continued. "Now everyone on the island thinks we're total sluts. I want to die!"

"It's like what your dad thinks about me!" Sam realized. The words just popped out of her mouth, but as she said it she realized how true it was.

"What do you mean?" Becky demanded.

"I know you guys think those photos of me you saw were cool, but they weren't. I was stupid to pose for them. What's more, I knew it was stupid when I did it, but I did it anyway."

"Why?" Allie asked.

"I guess because I wanted Flash to like me," Sam admitted. "I didn't want him to think I was just a stupid, unsophisticated kid. I thought I could have this big modeling career, and that if I said no to those photos, he'd just drop me."

"Yeah, that's what we thought about Brent and Brian," Allie said morosely.

"Right," Sam agreed. "I didn't listen to my own best instincts, and I bet you guys didn't, either."

"Yeah," Allie murmured, looking at the rug. "I knew it was stupid . . ." Her voice trailed off.

"Me, too," Becky agreed grudgingly.

"Well, me, three," Sam said. "I guess the best thing we can all do now is hold our heads up high and not let what anybody thinks get to us. After all, *we* know we didn't really do anything so terrible. The kids you know will stop talking about you as soon as everyone finds something else to talk about, which will be soon," she assured them. "And, speaking for myself, from now on I'm going to make my decisions based on my own standards, and not what anybody else thinks I should or shouldn't do—or at least I'm going to try." Sam sighed.

"Did Dad fire you?" Allie asked.

"He started to," Sam said, "but Stephanie wanted to talk to him about it. My job hangs by a thread."

"We don't want you to go," Becky said. "I know sometimes we're kind of bratty and everything, but we kind of like having you around."

Sam smiled. "Thanks for the moral support."

"Sam?" said Mr. Jacobs. He stood in the twins' doorway. "Could you come downstairs?"

Sam looked back at the twins as she followed their father out of the room. Both of them held up crossed fingers, their faces full of hope.

"Stephanie and I have had quite a discussion about this," Mr. Jacobs began once they were in the den again. He cleared his throat. "And Stephanie thinks that to have you just disappear from the twins' lives at this point would do more harm than good. They are very attached to you."

"Oh, and I'm attached to them!" Sam assured him. She quickly vowed never to refer to them as monsters again, if only she could keep her job.

"I also pointed out that perhaps Dan was jumping to conclusions about you," Stephanie said in a kind voice. "A picture can be worth a thousand words, but not all those words are necessarily true," she said.

Sam smiled at her gratefully. "You're absolutely right! I just . . . thank you for believing me," was all Sam could say.

"So," Mr. Jacobs concluded, "I've decided not to fire you. You are, however, on probation as far as I'm concerned."

"I understand!" Sam said. "I won't let you down."

"Well, good," Mr. Jacobs said, obviously embarrassed. "Let's just put this behind us, then. I'm, uh, going to go talk to the girls. Excuse me."

Sam sat down on the couch next to Stephanie. "I can't thank you enough for saving my job," she said. "I was really terrified!"

Stephanie laughed. "You're welcome, but in addition to the fact that I really didn't think he should fire you, I confess to having ulterior motives. If you leave, I'll have to deal with the twins all by myself. Now, that's a *really* terrifying thought!"

ELEVEN

"So, that's the whole story," Sam concluded. "I still have a job, but Flash has these sleazoid photos of me. And everyone on Sunset Island can see them!"

It was later that evening at the Play Café, and Sam was relating the gruesome details of her misadventures to Emma and Carrie.

"I'm so glad that Mr. Jacobs didn't fire you," Carrie said. She remembered only too well how she had felt when Graham and Claudia almost fired her for sneaking out to the midnight beach party with Billy. "Thank God Stephanie was on your side."

"No kidding," Sam agreed. "If it hadn't been for her I would be on the next plane back to Kansas." She shuddered to think of that. It was the worst possible thing that could happen to her.

Emma jabbed her straw angrily through the ice at the bottom of her glass of Coke. "I knew Flash was a lowlife! I just knew it!"

"Please," said Sam. "'I told you so' are the last words I need to hear."

"But doesn't it make you crazy that he's got those pictures of you?" Emma protested.

"Yes, it makes me crazy," Sam said. "But what am I supposed to do about it? You think he's likely to give them back just because I ask nicely? After the scene I made at Sugarloaf he's probably planning to show them at the Sunset Gallery, and then sell them to the highest bidder."

"I knew you shouldn't have signed that release," Emma sighed.

Sam looked at Carrie. "If she says 'I knew it' one more time, I'm going to kill her."

"I'm sorry," Emma apologized. "It's just that I'm mad at myself. I should have stopped you."

"That's how I feel, too," Carrie admitted.

"You guys," Sam said, "it was my decision. A stupid one, I grant you, but all mine." Sam shook her head. "How could I have taken seriously a grown man who wears all those chains and refers to himself as the Flashman?"

"Yeah, he should call himself the Fleshman!" Carrie said.

The girls were still snickering when Patsi came over to their table.

"Only an hour left to my shift, only an hour left to my shift . . . if I keep repeating that to myself, I might make it till midnight."

"Tough night?" Carrie sympathized with the harried waitress.

"Every night in here is a tough night." Patsi sighed. "Anyway, I seem to have become a service for the lovelorn," she said, handing Sam a folded-up paper napkin. "A certain hunky somebody asked me to deliver this to you. Can I leave your check at the same time, or would that ruin the moment?"

While Patsi scribbled the total on their check, Sam unfolded the napkin and read it quickly. It said, *Sam—I'm out in back looking at the stars. Join me? Pres.*

"Let me guess," said Carrie. "Does that note have a Southern accent?"

Sam smiled. "He's outside. I'll be right back."

Sam made her way through the throngs of kids in the club and went outside. The silence of the night was in startling contrast to the cacophony inside the café.

"Hi," Sam said when she saw Pres all by himself, sitting on a boulder.

"Hey," Pres answered softly. "Nice night."

Sam sat down next to him.

"I called your place and one of the girls said you were here," Pres said. "Of course, she made me promise to come over soon and give her a ride on the motorcycle before she'd tell me," he added.

"Why didn't you come in?" Sam asked.

Pres shrugged. "I'm not in the mood for that zoo, I guess. Besides, I wanted to talk to you alone."

"Okay," Sam said.

Pres just stared up into the night sky. "I wrote a new song," he said finally.

"Is that what you wanted to tell me? Not that I'm not happy for you, but it could have waited."

Presley chuckled and ran his hand through his hair. "You are a hard one, woman. No, I wanted to talk to you about this weekend."

"Look, I already told you—" Sam began.

"I got your message, loud and clear," Pres said, holding up a hand to stop Sam. "I just wanted you to know that I'm not taking Kristy. I'm not taking anyone."

"Well, good," said Sam. "I'm sure there'll be plenty of nubile young things panting after you in Bangor—"

Pres held a finger to his lips to shush Sam. "You know, if I didn't like you so much, you would make me crazier than a coyote on loco weed."

"A coyote on loco weed?" Sam repeated. "No one actually talks that way, do they?"

"What I'm tryin' to say, you nut, is that if I'm not spendin' the weekend with you, then I'm spendin' it without the pleasure of female company."

"Really?" Sam asked, flattered in spite of herself.

Pres nodded. "I still think it's too early to make any kind of promises, but I do take gettin' to know you seriously, and I wanted you to know that."

"What about Kristy?" Sam asked.

"Why go lookin' to eat hamburger when you got a steak waitin' at the table?"

"Do you often compare girls to food?" Sam asked. "It's kind of obnoxious."

"Point taken," Pres conceded. "Sometimes the words don't come out right, but the thought was sincere."

"Is that an apology?" Sam asked.

"Yes." Pres laughed. "That's an apology."

"Well, then, apology accepted," Sam said with a smile.

Pres leaned close and kissed her until she was breathless.

"So I'll see you when I get back?" Pres asked.

"Okay," Sam said nonchalantly.

Sam walked back into the café with a huge grin on her face.

"Well, you look like the cat who ate the canary," Carrie said.

"Mmmm," was Sam's response. She leaned her chin on her hand and stared into space.

"She likes Pres again," Carrie said to Emma.

"Mmmm," Sam murmured dreamily.

"I guess you worked it out about not going away with him for the weekend," Carrie continued. "I decided not to go with Billy, either, and he was very cool about it. He said we have plenty of time to get to know each other."

"Mmmm," Sam said again.

Carrie looked at Emma. "She appears to be planet-hopping somewhere out there in the galaxy."

"I'll say," Emma agreed. "Earth to Sam! Earth to Sam!" she called. Sam finally looked in Emma's direction. "Love is grand and all, but what are you going to do about Flash spreading your pictures all over the world?"

Sam came crashing back to earth. "I don't know. Nothing, I guess."

Just then a large, muscular guy named Butchie came into the café with his entourage of male hangers-on. Butchie had had it in for the girls ever since Carrie humiliated him in a pool tournament.

"Look what the wind just blew in," Carrie said.

Butchie and his three friends spied the girls and started nudging one another, laughing and pointing toward the girls' table. Butchie staggered as he leaned over to talk to one of the other guys, who steadied him so that he didn't fall.

"I think they're talking about us," Carrie said.

"I think they're drunk," Sam murmured.

"I already paid Patsi. Let's get out of here," Emma said tersely.

"You don't have to pay for me," Sam said. "I'm perfectly capable of paying for myself—"

"Fine," Emma said, sliding out of the booth. "Pay me back outside."

The girls tried to walk past Butchie and his friends, but Butchie blocked the front door of the café.

"Yo, Big Red!" Butchie said in a booming voice. "Good to see you again."

"Hi," Sam said curtly as she tried to edge around him.

"I hardly recognized you with your clothes on!" Butchie guffawed.

"Yeah," his friend Larry agreed, moving next to Butchie to block the door. "Imagine finding out that Big Red does porn! That shot of you in the leopard-print see-through thing was hot stuff, babe!"

To Sam's horror, the noisy café had silenced. Almost everyone was watching her. There were murmurs, people asking one another what Butchie and his friends were talking about. They waited to see what Sam would do.

"Get out of my way," Sam said.

"Or we'll call the manager," Emma added.

"Or you'll call the manager?" Butchie said in a falsetto voice full of mock horror. "Oooo, we're very frightened!" He stared insolently at Sam again, licking his lips obscenely. "Hey, you and me could have a great time," he bellowed drunkenly. "I'm just as easy as you are!"

Butchie held out his arms to Sam, and she saw him sway. She pushed past him with all her might. In his drunkenness he was caught off balance, and as he staggered sideways toward Larry, all three girls rushed out the door.

They ran down the block, into the protective

shadows, until all three of them were panting from the chilly night air and the fear.

"Oh my God, oh my God," Sam kept saying, bending over and panting with her hands on her knees.

Carrie recovered first, and she half dragged Sam and Emma over to the deserted front porch of the Sunset Gallery. They all sat down on the front step, trying to recover.

"I was really scared," Emma admitted.

"They saw my pictures!" Sam wailed. "Those disgusting pigs saw those photos of me! Everyone on the whole island will know now. What am I going to do?"

Emma stared at her. "No offense, Sam, but that's what I've been trying and trying to tell you! You've been acting so blasé, like this isn't going to ruin your reputation! I realize you're very experienced, and you don't care what people think—"

"Oh, shut up, Emma!" Sam cried. "I am not very experienced! I'm just as much of a virgin as you are."

Emma and Carrie stared at her.

"But I thought you said—" Carrie began.

"I never said," Sam interrupted. "You just assumed."

"But the way you talk, the way you act . . ." Emma said.

"So what about it?" Sam asked belligerently, close to tears. "You didn't actually expect me to do it for the first time with one of the yokels in Junction, did you?"

"I guess not," Emma said.

"Wow, this is funny," Carrie said. "Who would have thought that it would turn out that I'm more experienced than both of you? I'm the one who's had only one boyfriend before Billy, and I'm not even sleeping with Billy!"

"Yet," Emma added.

"What am I going to do?" Sam whispered. "This is the worst thing that ever happened to me!"

"Should I talk to Jane?" Emma asked. "After all, she's a really terrific lawyer. Maybe there's some way to get the negatives back from Flash."

"I'd feel like such an idiot telling Jane what I did," Sam said.

"Yeah, but like you said, now that Butchie and his friends have seen the photos, soon the whole island will know."

"I know the first thing I'm going to do," Sam said, standing up decisively. "I'm going over to Victor's and I'm going to tear those photos down."

"But as long as he's got the negatives he can just put more up," Emma pointed out.

"I don't care. I'm not going to stand still for this."

The three girls got into the Templetons' Porsche, which Carrie had borrowed for the evening, and they quickly drove over to Victor's.

"If the room upstairs is private, how are we going to get in without a membership card or something?" Carrie asked nervously as they rushed through the front door.

"I think they'll recognize me," Sam said grimly. They spotted stairs and Sam headed for them.

"Hey, you can't go up there!" the maître d' yelled as the girls ran past him. Fortunately they were quicker than he was.

Sam pushed open the door at the top of the stairs, and the girls entered a dimly lit room. As their eyes adjusted to the light, they could see a small stage in the front of the room, where a girl in a tiny sequined bikini was dancing around to blasting music. Just as the girl was taking off her bikini top, a hand fell on Sam's shoulder.

"You a member?" the deep voice of the bouncer growled.

Sam turned around and the bouncer saw her face.

"Hey, it's you!" he said, his meaty face lighting up. He turned to look over his right shoulder. The girls' gazes followed his. There on the wall was picture after picture of Sam.

"Oh, my," Emma breathed.

"No membership card needed, doll!" the bouncer said with a big grin.

"Look, I can level with you?" Sam asked him.

"Ivan's the name," he said. "Go ahead and level."

"Ivan, I didn't know those pictures were going to be used like this. I'm only eighteen. I've got a summer job as an au pair on the island. My employer saw those shots and almost fired me. If those pictures stay up in here it will probably ruin my reputation and maybe my entire life."

Ivan scratched at his stubbly beard. "You mean Flash just stuck these photos up here without even telling you? That's lame, man."

"I agree," Sam said. "So would you let me take them down?"

"Let you? I'll help you!" He turned around and started pulling the photos from the wall. Sam, Carrie, and Emma joined in. "I've got a sister who's sixteen," Ivan said, ripping off another picture. "I'd kill Flash if he got hold of her."

Finally all the pictures were taken down, and Ivan handed them to Sam.

"Will you get in trouble with the owner?" Sam asked him.

"I'm the manager of this room. I rent it from the guy who owns the restaurant, so I guess you could say I'm the owner."

Sam thanked Ivan profusely and the girls ran back to Carrie's car with the photos.

"He was really nice," Carrie said. "What a great guy."

"Wow, Sam, these photos!" Emma said as she looked at a particularly sleazy one.

"Oh God, they're even worse than I thought," Sam cried. She hadn't really looked at them until now. Under the hot studio lights the lingerie Flash had picked for her was completely transparent. "He knew they'd look like this," she said angrily. And the angles he'd photographed her from—no wonder Mr. Jacobs had been horrified. Sam was mortified.

"Who's up for a bonfire on the beach?" she asked, "I know just what we can use for fuel!"

TWELVE

Sam had decided she was going to be the world's greatest au pair, at least for a while. She hadn't forgotten Mr. Jacobs's words—"as far as I'm concerned, you're on probation"— and she took them seriously. So she had volunteered to stay with the twins on Thursday night so that Mr. Jacobs could go out with Stephanie, and she had planned lots of fun activities for the girls during the day. Sam didn't mind lying low—the last thing she wanted to do was to run into Butchie and his friends, or anyone else who might have seen those photographs.

She had talked with Emma several times about the situation with Flash. Emma had told Jane everything, and Sam had even had a conversation with Jane on the phone so that Jane could make sure she had all the facts correct. Jane had said she'd call Sam as soon as she had any news.

On Friday afternoon, Jane finally called. The twins were playing a Graham Perry CD as loud as was humanly possible, and they were screaming the lyrics along with him even louder than that.

"Hello?" Sam screamed into the phone.

"Hi, Sam, it's Jane Hewitt."

"Just a sec, Jane," Sam said. She ran down the hall to the twins' bedroom. "Turn that down. I'm trying to talk on the phone!" Sam yelled.

In response, Becky turned the music up even louder. Sam ran back to the phone and pulled the long extension cord into her room, where she shut the door.

"Sorry, Jane," Sam said.

"No problem. I think I have some good news for you," Jane said. "First I tried getting the negatives from your friend Flash, but he said you signed a release and he didn't have to give them up, which unfortunately is true."

"That's not good news," Sam said glumly.

"There's more," Jane assured her. "Then I told him you were ready, willing, and able to report him to Universal Models, and he's really concerned that you'll do it. He says he'll give you the negatives plus the release you signed if you agree not to report his behavior."

"But I want to report him!" Sam protested.

"Well, that's a choice you're going to have to make," Jane said. "I think it's the best deal you're going to get, frankly."

"What's to stop me from getting the stuff and then going to Universal with the truth, anyway?" Sam asked.

"Nothing," Jane said. "It's your call. Just let me know what you want me to tell him."

"I have to think about it," Sam said. She thanked Jane for her help and hung up. "Now what do I do?" Sam said out loud. She could hear the twins jumping around in their room—the whole house was shaking. She marched down the hall, went in, and turned off the music.

"Hey!" Becky protested.

"That was absolutely rotten, turning the music up when I told you I had a phone call," Sam fumed.

Becky shrugged. Allie just continued polishing her toenails. Some of the red polish had spilled onto the lacquered white top of the nightstand.

"Look what you're doing!" Sam yelled, pointing to the nightstand. Allie took a halfhearted swipe at it, but only smeared the red polish over the lacquered wood.

"You know what?" Sam asked. "You two are acting like spoiled brats."

"So?" Becky said. "You're not our mother."

"What happened to how you wanted me around? What happened to how you were going to try to be more responsible for your behavior?" Sam demanded.

In answer to that Becky just turned the music on again and increased the volume to a deafening pitch.

"I give up!" Sam screamed, and stormed out of their room. She threw herself down on her bed. "You're monsters!" Sam screamed at the top of her lungs. "You're not human!"

Then a thought hit Sam. She had always thought that the twins thought being called "the monsters" was cool. But maybe deep down they didn't. Maybe they acted like monsters because that's what everyone told them they were.

And then she thought about herself, and the assumptions people like Butchie and Flash had made about her because of her behavior. But those assumptions weren't true. And if she had been honest with herself in the first place, the whole mess never would have happened. Suddenly she knew just what she had to do about Flash. She sat up and quickly dialed Jane Hewitt's number.

"Hello, Jane? It's Sam."

"Hi. Did you want Emma?" Jane asked. "She's giving Katie a bath."

"No, I called about the thing with Flash." Sam said. "Tell him I agree to his terms. If he give me the negatives and the release I won't report him to Universal Models."

"You're sure that's how you want to do it?" Jane asked.

"I'm sure," Sam answered.

"In that case I'll call him and arrange to get the negatives," Jane said. "Sam, I think you're doing the right thing."

"Thanks." Sam hung up and was about to make another call when the phone rang.

"Hi, this is Pam Winslow."

"Oh, hi, Pam. It's Samantha Bridges."

"Hi there, Sam," Pam said in a weary voice. "I'm calling because I need to fit some extra outfits on the twins for the fashion show tomorrow. One of my models for Savannah's, a girl named Daphne, seems to be too sick to be in the show."

"What happened to her?" Sam asked.

"I don't know. Her mom called, but she

didn't give any details. Anyway, I thought the twins could do her casual wear. She was modeling one of the bridesmaids' dresses in the wedding finale, but I'll have to find someone else for that. Can you possibly bring them over to Savannah's?"

"Now?" Sam asked.

"Please?" Pam said. "I'm really going crazy here."

"Okay," Sam agreed.

Sam told the twins about Pam's phone call, and they were out the door in two minutes. Sam couldn't help noticing that when it came to anything having to do with the fashion show, the twins were suddenly the most malleable girls in the world.

"You guys are really excited about this, aren't you?" Sam said to them on the way over to the store.

"We really want to be good," Allie said.

"We don't want to mess up or anything," Becky added.

"And we want to show all those kids who are laughing at us about—you know—that we're too cool to let them bother us."

Sam realized that although she'd been shuttling the twins all over the island, she hadn't really been talking to them about what was on their minds. And it wasn't as if they had an older sister or a mother to talk to. They certainly weren't opening up to Stephanie yet.

"Hi, girls. Thanks for getting here so quickly," Pam said when they arrived at Savannah's. "Go right back to the dressing room." When the twins had left Pam sagged into a chair and rubbed her temples.

"Rough day?" Sam asked sympathetically.

"This fashion show has been the biggest nightmare—just one thing after another," Pam admitted. "I've redone the finale, but the wedding gown I'm using can't compare to Kimmy's," she said. "And Daphne was modeling the bridal gown. She was hardly my first choice, but her aunt insisted. . . . Anyway, it's already been altered to fit her. Obviously the twins are too young, not that the gown would fit them, anyway. Finding a new model now . . ." Pam just shook her head. "I suppose it would be pointless for me to try asking you one last time to be in the fashion show. I do understand your concern about starting your professional career, but—"

"Yes," said Sam.

"Pardon me?" Pam asked.

"I said yes, I'll be in the fashion show. If you'll still have me, that is."

Like magic the exhaustion left Pam's face. "I don't even care why you changed your mind, so don't tell me," she said, jumping up from her chair. Then she got an idea. "I can call Kimmy and get the gorgeous wedding gown back! We can do the original finale! This will be spectacular! Say you can stay now so we can do the fittings and change the finale," Pam pleaded. "I'll call Kimmy."

"I will," Sam said, "but I need to make a phone call first." While she'd been driving, she'd come up with an incredible idea. True, it depended on asking Kristy Powell for help, but Sam was willing to swallow her pride. Her plan was more important.

Sam went outside and found a telephone, then called information and asked for Kristy Powell's phone number. Kristy answered on the second ring. Certainly she was surprised to hear from Sam, but she listened to everything Sam had to say, and in the end she agreed to Sam's plan.

The next three hours were a whirlwind of fittings. The twins were thrilled that Sam was going to be in the fashion show with them. They brought her water when she got thirsty, they gave their opinion when she practiced walking, twirling, and posing in the wedding gown, and they gave her moral support. By the time they were done all three of them were starved. Since they knew Mr. Jacobs was going out to dinner with Stephanie, they decided to dine on hot-fudge sundaes at the local ice cream parlor. Sam ate more than both twins put together, which they found hysterically funny. They teased her that she'd burst out of the wedding gown the next day.

The phone was ringing when they got home. Sam grabbed it quickly and fell, exhausted, into a chair.

"Hi, it's Emma. I've got news!"

"Me, too," Sam said. "I decided to be in that fashion show after all."

"That's great!" Emma said. "It's tomorrow, isn't it? I saw a flyer at the Cheap Boutique."

"Uh-huh," said Sam. "Can you come?"

"Wouldn't miss it," Emma said. "I'm sure Carrie will come, too. How about if I bring you the negatives of your photos then?"

"Jane got them?" Sam screamed.

"Belinda just brought them over. She seemed totally different from the mean-looking girl who did your makeup at that first shoot," Emma said. "She said she was leaving the island. She stopped to say good-bye to Flash, and he handed them all to her to give you. That creep couldn't even do that much himself!"

"I don't care. I don't care. I'm just so happy you have them!" Sam sang out. "Did Belinda say where she was going?"

"I don't know. She left you a note. It's on top of the negatives," Emma said.

"And you didn't read it?" Sam asked. "Is it sealed or something?"

"No, it's just a folded piece of paper with your name on it. I didn't read it because it isn't mine," Emma explained.

"You're such a good girl, Emma," Sam teased.

"Hey, watch it or I'll keep one of these negatives," Emma laughed. "I'll call Carrie about tomorrow," she added. "We'll be rooting for you!"

THIRTEEN

The next day dawned bright and sunny. Sam was surprisingly nervous. She went downstairs to make the twins breakfast, and found them already eating eggs they'd scrambled themselves.

"Well, well. I knew you had it in you," she said approvingly. "Is your dad up?"

"He didn't come home," Becky said with a smirk on her face. "You know what that means," she added.

"Yeah, what a hypocrite," Allie said. "All that stuff about how no one who isn't married stays in the same room in this house."

Sam had no comeback to that observation. It seemed pretty hypocritical to her, too. She poured herself a cup of coffee and sat at the breakfast table.

"I'm just surprised he didn't let me know," Sam said. "I hope everything's okay."

"Oh, he called last night," Allie said, scarfing down another mouthful of eggs. "You were dead to the world. He said he and Stephanie would meet us at the fashion show. We made you some eggs," she added shyly.

It was the first time that the twins had ever made her a meal, so although the last thing her nervous stomach wanted was eggs, she accepted a plateful with feigned enthusiasm.

The twins actually helped Sam clean up from breakfast, and then all three of them hurried to shower and dress. They had to be there two hours before the show, to go over some final plans and to have their makeup professionally done.

A stage had been set up in the middle of Sunset Square mall. Four guys were busy setting up hundreds of folding chairs when the twins and Sam arrived. Sam's stomach started fluttering again as she pictured herself walking across that stage and down the runway in a wedding gown. She pictured herself tripping over the train and falling into the crowd. *No. Think positively*, she told herself, and hurried into Savannah's, where all the models were being made up.

"Sam! Over here!" Pamela called when Sam came in with the twins. The three made their way through the crowd of nervous models, stylists, designers, and various assistants running to and fro. "Girls, go to table four," Pam said to the twins checking something off on her master list, which was attached to a clipboard. "They're all numbered. Cheryl is doing your makeup."

"Okay," the twins agreed happily, and rushed to where they were supposed to be.

"This is Suki. She's going to be doing your makeup and helping you into the wedding gown," Pam told Sam, introducing a pretty, petite Asian girl with beautiful long black hair.

"Hi," said Suki. "I staked out a quiet corner in the back. Come on, I'll show you."

"I'm really excited," Sam said as Suki started to do her pale makeup base.

"I saw the gown you're modeling," Suki said. "I'd love to get married in something like that—although I'm so little that it would swallow me up."

"Are you engaged?" Sam asked as Suki feathered in Sam's eyebrows.

"Not me, fortunately," she replied. "I just arrived on the island yesterday, and the first thing I did was go to the beach. The beach was hot, but the guys I saw were even hotter!"

"This is a guy-watching paradise," Sam agreed.

"I freelance as a makeup artist and stylist all over the place," Suki said. "Pam hires me a lot. This is by far the most gorgeous place she's ever brought me to. I'd love to stay for a while, if I could find some work."

"Yeah, that's tough," Sam said. "Most of the jobs get hooked up in the spring."

"Well, I might be onto something," Suki said eagerly, dabbing Sam's eyelids with a pale pink eyeshadow. "I met this guy named Leonard something on the beach, and he told me his boss is a photographer for Universal Models, and he needs a makeup artist!"

"Don't tell me. His name is Flash Hathaway," Sam groaned.

"You know him?" Suki asked.

"The guy is really a sleazeball," Sam said. She didn't want to go into what had happened between her and Flash; she just hoped that Suki would take her word for it.

"Well, does he really work for Universal?" Suki asked.

"Yeah," Sam admitted.

"That's good enough for me!" Suki said, adding a line of brown eyeliner under Sam's eyes. "Believe me, I can take care of myself," she assured Sam.

"Just be careful," Sam warned her.

A half-hour later Suki was done with Sam's makeup. She handed Sam a mirror to check out the results.

"Wow!" was all Sam could say. Suki had done Sam's face in pale, muted tones. Her eyelids and cheeks and lips were painted a pale, matte pink, and her skin looked like porcelain.

"*Très* bridal, don't you think?" Suki asked with a grin.

"*Très!*" Sam agreed with a laugh.

"I've got to go find this other model I'm supposed to do next," Suki said. "I'll catch you later."

The twins came running over to Sam, their faces beaming.

"How do we look?" they demanded.

"Fabulous!" Sam exclaimed. The makeup artist had given the twins a completely natural look. They looked like themselves, only better. Which was terrific, since they were pretty to start with.

"She showed us what colors to use and stuff," Allie said.

"Well, I love it," Sam told them. "Maybe later we can buy you some new makeup and I can help you guys do it yourselves."

"Ladies! Ladies! Can I have your attention,

please?" Pamela called over the cacophony. "You'll find the running order of the show posted on both sides of the stage. Remember that you line up backstage behind the model who goes on before you, so that you're always prepared for your entrances. Your clothes will be on the racks in order, and the dressers will be standing by to help you with any quick changes. Once your makeup is done, please go outside and wait backstage. Have a wonderful time!"

There was a smattering of nervous applause, then everyone went back to whatever they'd been in the middle of doing.

"Let's get you girls backstage," a harried-looking assistant with a clipboard told the twins. "You're on third in Savannah's sportswear," she noted, "then you're on again thirteenth, and again twenty-fifth," she noted. The twins beamed. They were the only ones who had three changes of clothing.

"You won't be able to watch us!" Allie pouted to Sam.

"I know, I wish I could," Sam said. "But your dad and Stephanie will be out there. Break a leg!" she added, giving them both a hug.

"Break a leg?" Becky repeated.

"It's show biz talk," Sam laughed. "It means good luck!"

Sam wandered outside to the backstage area, but she kept out the way. Since she wasn't on until the very end, she wasn't in any hurry. She did manage to peek out at one point. She was amazed by the size of the crowd—it looked like everyone on the island was out there. She saw Carrie and Emma sitting in the fifth row. Farther back she saw Mr. Jacobs and Stephanie. Mr. Jacobs had a camera around his neck.

The show finally started. Sam could hear Pam's voice through the sound system as she welcomed everyone to the Sunset Island fashion show.

The assistants got the first few models in line backstage, and then the first model made her way through the curtain and out onto the stage to a burst of applause. Soon it was the twins' turn. One entered from the right, and the other came in from the left. They were wearing casual outfits that were the same cut but different colors. The audience murmured its approval of the cute lookalike twins parading across the stage, and Sam smiled happily for them from her position backstage.

About halfway through the show Suki found Sam and pulled her toward the clothes rack. "Come on," she whispered. "We've got to get you into the gown. I got stuck with a girl whose button popped off."

"I'm a little nervous," Sam confessed as Suki slid the bottom layer of plain white silk over Sam's head.

"You'll knock 'em dead," Suki said absently, straightening out the silk slip to make sure it hung correctly.

"Do you know that Pam told me this dress is worth ten thousand dollars?" Sam whispered. "Is that amazing or what?"

"Amazing," Suki said, frowning. "Didn't Pam tell you to wear a strapless bra with this?" she asked.

Sam shook her head. "Neither one of us thought the straps showed when I tried the dress on yesterday," she said. "Anyway, I don't own a strapless bra. I could just leave it off completely," she suggested.

"I don't think that's exactly the blushing bride look," Suki said. "Let me see if I can find a strapless bra back here somewhere."

Suki ran off, and Sam stood there in the silk slip. The show was continuing at a fast pace. It seemed to Sam that they were more than three-quarters of the way through, and still Suki hadn't returned.

When the twins walked out in their third

outfit, Sam started to panic. She knew there were only five models left before the wedding finale. With trembling fingers she started unpinning the gown from its hanger. Just then Suki ran back over to her.

"Success!" she whispered, handing Sam the strapless bra. "Remind me that belongs to Joan Shey," she said. Sam donned the bra quickly, and fortunately it fit. Suki helped her into the other three pieces of the silk-and-lace gown, then set a garland of baby's breath on Sam's hair. From the garland floated a veil edged in lace that billowed over Sam's hair and down the back of the wedding gown. Suki spun Sam around so that she could see herself in the three-way mirror.

And Sam, who had always found formal wedding gowns kind of sappy, instantly changed her mind. *Maybe someday,* she thought to herself, smiling at her reflection, *as long as the someday is far, far away.*

"Quick! Time to get in line!" Suki whispered, handing Sam her bouquet of white and pink flowers. Already waiting in line were the two models dressed as bridesmaids, in pink-and-white polka-dot off-the-shoulder gowns trimmed with lace, and the maid of honor, in pink raw silk with a waistband made of the same lace as was in

Sam's gown. Sam took one step toward the line and stopped dead in her tracks.

"My shoes!" Sam whispered frantically. She lifted up the bottom of the wedding gown. There on her feet were red cowboy boots.

"Where are they?" Suki asked, exasperated.

"I thought you had them!" Sam said.

"Didn't you try on shoes yesterday when they fitted the gown?" Suki asked in horror.

"I think we all forgot," Sam said. "Everything was so rushed."

"What's the very best thing about summer?" Pam was saying from the stage. "Summer weddings, of course. From Savannah's designer collection we have Debbie and Maia in summery, sweet bridesmaids' dresses of polkadot silk . . ."

The two models walked out onto the stage, and the model dressed as the maid of honor was looking around frantically for Sam.

"What size?" Suki asked Sam quickly, ready to take off her own summer flats. At least they were white.

"Ten," Sam admitted. Suki winced. "I'm sorry! I'm tall! I've got big feet!"

"I need a size-ten shoe for Sam, quick!" Suki asked in the loudest stage whisper possible.

"Oh, thanks, tell the whole world," Sam

muttered. All around her, girls were shrugging. No one wore a ten.

"And now here's Leslie, our beautiful maid of honor," Pamela was saying from the stage.

Suki stared at Sam, Sam stared at Suki, and finally Sam just shrugged. "Maybe they won't show."

"Yeah, and maybe Pam will never hire me again," Suki moaned.

"To finish our show today, a beautiful bride in a one-of-a-kind gown," Pam said.

Sam took a deep breath and walked through the curtains out onto the stage. She could hear people oohing and aahing as they saw her in the gorgeous gown. Emma and Carrie started applauding, and then everyone else did, too. As Pam's narration continued, Sam tried to move ethereally, which she did not find easy in cowboy boots. Pam got to the point in her narration where Sam was supposed to pivot on the runway that extended out into the audience. Her train floating behind her, Sam did the pivot the way Pam had showed her the day before—cross the legs at the ankles, and pivot in a circle in one swift, smooth move. Sam did it, but there was no way she could do it without lifting the bottom of the gown the tiniest bit, or she would have tripped herself. At that moment the audience saw the cowboy boots. Pam saw the cowboy boots. And Sam knew that everyone was staring at the cowboy boots.

"You, too, can be a beautiful bride," Pam continued after faltering for a second, "in a gown designed especially, exclusively for you. After all, there is no other bride quite like you. Savannah's believes in celebrating the unique!"

Sam winked at the audience, and lifted the bottom of the wedding gown a little higher. Everyone laughed and applauded as Sam made her way off the stage.

Sam just stood there shaking while Suki pulled the wedding gown off. "This is one fashion show I will never forget," Suki said, arranging the gown carefully on its hanger as Sam threw on the T-shirt and jeans she'd arrived in.

As Sam brushed out her hair she could hear Pam wrap up the narration. Everyone applauded heartily, and the whole thing was finally over.

"Sam!" Pam called to Sam when she saw her backstage.

"I'm sorry," Sam said in a rush. "We forgot about shoes yesterday! I didn't even think about it! I—"

"Stop!" Pam said, laughing. "I have to admit,

you stumped me for a moment, but then I thought up that bit about celebrating the unique—I'm sure everyone thinks we planned it!"

"Oh, thank God!" Sam said. "I was so worried!"

"Well, you can stop worrying. I think it made the show. I may call you sometime if I'm doing another show in this part of the country. I'd like to use you again, if you're interested."

"I'd love to!" Sam said.

The twins ran over and told her they were going to find their dad, so Sam collected her stuff and went out to locate her friends.

"Wow, you were terrific!" Carrie cried, hugging Sam hard.

"I agree!" Emma said, adding her hug to Carrie's. "And the cowboy boots—what a wonderful, funny touch!"

"It was so you," Carrie laughed. "Whoever thought of it?"

"A quirk of fate," Sam said. "I'll tell you about it sometime."

"I've got a little present for you," Emma said, handing Sam a large envelope full of photo negatives.

"Thank you, thank you, thank you," Sam said, kissing the envelope.

"I know you made a deal," Emma said. "I just wish you felt like you could break your word and call Universal Models to report Flash anyway."

"Yeah," said Carrie. "I just can't stand the thought that he'll keep getting away with it."

"Maybe he won't," Sam said. She saw Kristy out of the corner of her eye. "Excuse me a sec," she said.

Carrie and Emma looked shocked as Sam walked quickly over to Kristy, who nodded her head and handed Sam a newspaper. They watched as Sam scanned something in the paper, and then headed back over to her two friends, Kristy in tow.

"Read Kristy's column in today's *Breaker*," Sam said, thrusting the paper at her friends.

What gold-chain-wearing photographer-about-town is coercing girls on the island into taking their clothes off by promising them mega-careers in modeling? Quite a few girls have been taken in by this creep, who tries to tell them that his type of sleazy shots are standard operating procedure in the professional modeling world. Well, girls, he's a liar, so beware! Watch out, Mr. F. H., your prowling days on this island are over!

"This is fabulous!" Charlie screamed.

"It was really nice of you, Kristy," Emma added.

"He hit on me last year," Kristy said with a shrug. "I had to buy the negatives from him. When Sam called me yesterday—well, she made a good case for printing this. I mean, no girl has ever turned Flash in! He makes them all feel ashamed, or else he scares them into keeping their mouths shut. He's got this coming to him, for sure. I just about had to beg the editor to let me strip the copy and add this at the last minute, but it was worth it," she added.

"Now every girl on the island will know about Flash!" Sam crowed happily, "and I still kept my word."

"That's right." Carrie laughed. "You didn't say you wouldn't tell anybody; you just said you wouldn't tell Universal."

"Thanks again," Sam said to Kristy. "I owe you one."

"Good," said Kristy with a grin. "The one I want is Pres." She flipped her blond hair back over her shoulders and sauntered away.

"Hmmm, what does this make you two?" Carrie asked. "Friendly enemies?"

"Well, if she means she wants to fight me for

him, I say let the best woman win," Sam said. "Hey, we've got to go celebrate! How about tonight?"

"I told Kurt I'd go out in the taxi with him," Emma sighed. "He's working again."

"Cancel?" Sam suggested.

"I can't. I've told him three times I'd go with him, and then something always came up. Honestly, I love being with him, but it seems he's always working, so I hardly get the chance."

"Trouble in paradise?" Sam asked in mock horror, raising her eyebrows at Emma. "Let me catch Kristy. She can put it in her column next week."

"Don't you dare," Emma said, grabbing Sam as she pretended to run after Kristy.

"Okay, so let's go celebrate now," Sam suggested. "I'm starved! Our employers can't begrudge us time to go feed our faces, can they?"

As they walked toward the Play Café, a note fell out of the manila envelope of photo negatives that Sam was carrying. She picked it up and read it.

Dear Sam,
   I've decided to go home to Altoona for a while to figure out what I want to do. I'm

*thinking about going to school for art, or
maybe I'll hitchhike around the world, who
knows? Anyway, I know I kept saying I
didn't do it for you, but if it hadn't been for
you, I never would have had the guts to do it
at all. So thanks for being the one who
walked away.*

All the best,
Belinda

Sam smiled and slipped the note back into
the envelope.

"Something good?" Emma asked her softly.

"Something great," Sam said. "Come on,
let's go pig out."

Sam strode ahead in her bright red cowboy
boots, her head held high. After all, she was
the girl who had walked away.